Unrequited

MARTHA KEYES

Unrequited © 2022 by Martha Keyes. All Rights Reserved.
All rights reserved. No part of this book may be reproduced in any form or by any electronic or mechanical means including information storage and retrieval systems, without permission in writing from the author. The only exception is by a reviewer, who may quote short excerpts in a review.
Cover design by Martha Keyes.

This book is a work of fiction. Names, characters, places, and incidents are either products of the author's imagination or are used fictitiously. Any resemblance to actual persons, living or dead, events, or locales, is entirely coincidental.
Martha Keyes
http://www.marthakeyes.com

Chapter One

KENT, ENGLAND 1816

My long, brown hair, which was never particularly manageable, hung around my head like the mane of a lion, splintering off in every direction in a wild combination of kinks, curls, and straight pieces, as though each hair was afraid of going unnoticed.

My hair was always like this after one of my visits to the cove—the only place that could calm my nerves these days—and I had spent a great deal of time there today, returning to the Donovan's estate just before the arrival.

His arrival. The one I had been dreading and wanting for years. Seven years, in fact.

Diana, whose hair was already arranged becomingly, came up behind me and gently played with mine. "Marie Antoinette would have given anything to have your hair, Elena. No need for false pieces with a head of hair like yours."

I blew a puff of air upward with my lower lip, sending a curl fluttering in the air for a moment before it settled back into its chosen place on my forehead. "A shame I was born half a century too late."

The Scottish lilt to my words always sounded more pronounced when Diana was near. Her speech was so effortlessly elegant, as though she had been born and bred at Almack's. One would never have known we were educated at the same seminary, but I knew better than anyone that she could swear like a sailor under the right circumstances. She had grown up surrounded by them, after all.

"No matter," she said. "Tait can manage your hair."

I glanced at my own maid, Hitchen, in the mirror, and I saw a hint of hurt in her eyes. I felt for her; she had been given a difficult task, trying to make something presentable out of a young woman like myself. I tried to compliment her whenever I could, and normally, I was not so particular about my hair. But tonight . . . tonight, I would submit to Diana's maid, hoping she could achieve a miracle.

"You must be looking your very best for Mr. Bailey," Diana continued, going to look through my dresses. "Ah, yes. This green one will be perfect."

I blinked. Mr. Bailey. Yes, this should all be for *him*. It should be him I was thinking about when I pictured making an entrance at dinner, not Theo.

"Would you fetch Tait, Hitchen?" Diana said it like a command, infused with the sort of self-assurance she always used when speaking—much like her father. If she were to take over for Admiral Donovan, she would be regarded with every bit as much awe and obeyed with every bit as much haste by the sailors, for she spoke with the assumption that she would be heeded.

The thought of Diana's father made nerves tussle in my stomach. My own father, rest his soul, could hardly have chosen a more intimidating godfather for me. I had seen Admiral Donovan only a few times over the years, and I certainly owed him a great deal for allowing me to live at Blackwick Hall since finishing at Mrs. Westwood's Seminary for Fine Young Ladies four years ago, but I couldn't pretend I had ever been fully at ease in his company. Perhaps I would find it easier to maintain my confidence now that I was older.

Tait soon arrived, and I chuckled apologetically at the way her eyes widened at the sight of my hair.

"Help me," I said with a pleading that was only half-joking.

An hour later, I sat before the same mirror, but this time it was *my* eyes that grew wide. I was a changed creature. My hair was unrecognizable, a mixture of perfectly coiled ringlets and pomaded sleekness. The individual strands had been manipulated and orchestrated into a unity I had never before seen or thought possible.

Underneath, though, was still the same Elena. And though I could speak like a proper English lady, it was only with effort. My Scottish accent had not submitted to all of Mrs. Westwood's exertions; I hadn't allowed it to, but tonight I found myself regretting my stubbornness.

A woman's speech should be like music: composed, melodic, and precise.

Mrs. Westwood might not have succeeded in ridding me of my brogue, but her oft-repeated maxims were stamped upon my memory forever, reminding me how far I fell short of the ideal. *Far* short.

When Diana returned from dressing with the help of my maid, she inspected my hair with admiration, heaping praise upon Tait. The maid accepted it with an expressionless face and her hands folded before her, as though she was accustomed to working upon the hair of wild beasts and not Diana's.

With their help, I slipped into the evening dress Diana had chosen—an olive-green taffeta with a double, ruffled flounce and ruched sleeves.

"Mr. Bailey will be awestruck." Diana smiled and threaded my arm through hers, pulling me from the room.

I said nothing, for I saw little purpose in appealing to a man who was only here for two nights, but Diana was convinced tonight would be the start of something new for me.

For my part, I rather thought it might be *her* who struck him with awe. Or our friend Emmeline Aldridge. I was well enough looking, of course, and my dowry was substantial, but I lacked the dignified demeanor of a well-bred English lady. I had spent my childhood teasing coos and catching fish in Highland streams with my bare hands, not stitching samplers and practicing at the pianoforte.

But Diana had nipped any idea of her and Mr. Bailey in the bud when I had last suggested it, and I knew her well enough to believe that her father would not succeed if he tried to force such a thing. She had no thought of marrying, and with her father's large fortune, neither did she have any real need if she didn't wish to.

As we descended the stairs, I ignored the way my heart rapped against my chest. We reached the drawing room where everyone was congregating, and I noticed Admiral Donovan first, with his graying hair and fine dinner coat. He stood by the fireplace in conversation with a man whose back was to me. Above the man's well-tailored navy tailcoat collar, I could see a hint of his gray waistcoat, over which some locks of dark brown hair spilled.

Diana squeezed my arm and sent me a significant look, leaving no doubt about the man's identity: Mr. James Bailey, son of Admiral John Bailey, baronet. I smiled at Diana, and she pulled me in his direction, while my eyes searched the room for Theo.

Many families had gathered at Blackwick Hall to celebrate the end of the war and the return of Admiral Donovan and his son. I knew a pang of disappointment when my gaze failed to find Theo. Would he come down at all? Perhaps he was too tired from his journey.

My hair would look nothing like this in the morning if my first interaction with him was to be postponed until the breakfast table. It would be too unkind a fate. I needed our first meeting to overpower the mortifying memory I had left Theo with—the letter.

I would pretend not to remember that wretched, accursed letter. My cheeks grew hot at the mere thought.

Clandestine communication with the opposite sex is perhaps the most egregious error of all, for it leaves behind tangible incriminating evidence of its author's depravity.

Coming as they had on the heels of my own violation, these words had haunted me for years now. No fourteen-year-old girl should be allowed to make a written record of her thoughts, much less to send that record to the man who consumed those thoughts. It was an unforgivable oversight in the supervision due me as a young woman that I had managed to commit such an offense against my future self. The letter had been the ridiculous ramblings of an infatuated young girl, desperate to be loved, sunken in sorrow over her father's death, and awed by the life experience and relative wisdom of a handsome young man five years her senior. And it was the last thing he would remember of me.

Diana didn't know of the letter I had sent her brother to war with. No one did, save Theo and I, and I prayed Theo had forgotten all about it. He certainly hadn't bothered to write back, despite the pleadings I had included that he respond one way or the other, either giving me hope for the future or breaking my heart so that it could heal. Instead, he had left me to the slow and mortifying realization that he had not even cared for me enough to acknowledge it.

It had been seven years since then, though, and if he did remember . . . well, I hoped he would at least feel a small—or perhaps a bullet-sized—sliver of regret for paying so little heed to me all those years ago.

I shook myself back to the present as Diana performed the necessary introduction between Mr. Bailey and myself. Over the years, I had seen how people reacted to my brogue, and I made a quick decision.

"Good evening, Mr. Bailey. Welcome home, Admiral," I said in the accent Mrs. Westwood had drummed into me every day of my time at her seminary.

Diana glanced at me quizzically, but I avoided her gaze.

Mr. Bailey's gaze took me in, and an admiring glint entered his eyes. My confidence increased a measure, and within a couple of minutes, Diana had managed to pull her father away, leaving me alone with the gentleman.

He was an agreeable man with a ready smile and easy conversation, and I found myself happily occupied with him, and, as far as I could tell, he was as happily occupied with me.

The dinner bell rang, and I glanced to the doorway, heart stopping as my gaze met Theo's.

More times than I could count over the past seven years, I had persuaded myself that, in my girlish fascination with him, I had embellished Theo Donovan, making him into something superhuman, like a Greek god.

I had not.

If I had thought him handsome as a nineteen-year-old, fresh from taking his lieutenant's examination, nothing could have prepared me for Captain Theo Donovan at six-and-twenty. This was not the young boy with whom I had climbed trees, constructed forts of branches, and built fairy houses. He was fully a man now, blond hair glimmering in the candlelight, light blue eyes able to pierce me across the room, shoulders that struggled to fit into the confines of a dark tailcoat, and a jaw that must have been chiseled by every order given under his direction until it looked sharp enough to cut anyone who dared touch it.

He stood just inside the room, eyes set on me as fixedly as mine were on him. There was no denying the sequence of expressions that passed over his face—confusion, recognition, then admiration.

"May I accompany you in to dinner, Miss MacKinnon?"

Feeling the pulse of victory fill my chest, I pulled my eyes away, looking to Mr. Bailey and smiling. "I would like that very much."

He offered me his arm, and I took it gladly, feeling more confident than I had in years.

Yes, this was much better than I had hoped for—far better than stepping into a room with Diana. Let Theo see that I was the first one in the room with a gentleman to offer his escort, that Mr. Bailey could elicit my smile and my laugh with ease, that it had been a mistake to ignore me all those years ago. For I was no longer fourteen, with wild hair, a brogue difficult to understand, and a heart that lived and died by the attentions of Theo Donovan.

I was two-and-twenty now, and tonight, I would be every bit the English lady Mrs. Westwood had taught me to be.

Chapter Two

Between the Donovan family and the many neighbors invited to dinner, not a chair was empty at the grand dining table of Blackwick Hall that evening.

Mr. Bailey led me to a chair midway down the table, helping me into my seat before taking his own beside me. I met eyes with Diana, who smiled knowingly at me as she was assisted into her own seat.

Theo pulled out a chair for Emmeline Aldridge, and I felt a flicker of jealousy that belonged to seven years ago, so I turned my eyes elsewhere. On no account would I give anyone to think that I regarded Theo with anything but friendly affection. I would be the picture of amiable unconcern, and if he *did* bring up the past—heaven forbid—I would laugh it away as a relic of yore, or I would die trying. Besides, Emmeline was my friend. We had been at Mrs. Westwood's together, and I would force myself to be happy for her if she and Theo made a match of it.

I found Theo's eyes on me more than once over the course of the meal, and each occurrence sent a pulse of energy through my veins. For the most part, though, he was mindful of the people seated nearest him, conversing with them and laughing with them as he ought to do. All the Donovans had been brought up with the strictest ideas of etiquette—even if Diana and her rake of a brother, Valentine, did not always adhere to such ideas. Valentine had taken the seat farthest from his father and looked eager to be done with the entire ordeal. He was only celebrating the return of his older brother, Theo, I was sure, for he and his father had never seen eye to eye. As for Phineas, he sat opposite me, serene and quiet, as he generally was. The three brothers could hardly have been more different.

"I understand you are from Scotland, Miss MacKinnon," Mr. Bailey said. "Do you have family there still?"

"Not at the moment, no," I replied. "Neither of my parents are living, and all of my brothers have been serving in the army for some years."

Of course, it was possible that one—or all four of them—were already home now with the war being over, but as I had yet to receive word from any of them, I doubted it. I felt so disconnected from them after all our years apart. In the time since my father's death, I had seen only my oldest brother, Arthur, when he had come to Blackwick Hall to recover from a gunshot wound to the arm—the surgeon had instructed against sending him on the long and bumpy carriage ride back to Scotland. But even that had been three years ago.

"It has been a great while since your last visit there, then, I assume."

I nodded, trying to keep a tight rein on my accent, which I found particularly resistant when Scotland was the subject of discussion. "I came to England just after my father's death, and, with the war and the vast distance between here and my home, there has been no opportunity to return." Despite how often I returned to Benleith in my mind and dreams, Scotland felt more and more like a distant memory. So much of my life had been lived away from there now, first at Mrs. Westwood's seminary and then here at Blackwick Hall.

"A shame, that," he said. "I have heard many a tale of Scotland and its beauties." His eyes lingered on me just a moment longer than necessary.

I smiled politely, directing my gaze back at my food. I was uneasy speaking of my homeland. The English took a strange view of it—simultaneously romanticizing it and looking down upon it—but I felt uncomfortable with both approaches. For me, it was simply *home* and all that such a word encapsulated.

"When can we expect your mother?" I asked. Mr. Bailey and Lady Bailey were meeting at Blackwick before continuing their journey to visit friends in Sussex.

"Tomorrow, I hope," he said with his handsome smile. "I look forward to the two of you meeting one another."

My cheeks infused with warmth and my stomach with nerves at the thought of performing for Lady Bailey as Mrs. Westwood had taught me to do. I didn't know whether to be relieved or regretful when Mr. Bailey's attention was taken by the person to his left.

It was strange to mingle with so many people at the same time. It had been a great while since Blackwick Hall had seen such numbers. With the admiral and his sons all away and since Mrs. Donovan's death two years ago, the only company Diana and I had had was short visits from the neighbors. We hadn't been in a position to entertain and our outings had been limited to the nearby village, particularly during Mrs. Donovan's protracted illness and the period of mourning following her death.

I found I preferred quiet, informal dinners.

Admiral Donovan had once written, expressing his desire that Diana accept her elderly aunt to come act as a chaperone of sorts, but Diana had ignored the suggestion, just as she ignored anything she didn't particularly wish to do. If her father had been in a position to easily verify her obedience or ensure it, perhaps she would have heeded him, but he was far away and his letters both infrequent and delayed. I, on the other hand, couldn't imagine doing anything contrary to the admiral's orders, but I was more than happy to follow Diana's lead. She never batted an eye when I disappeared for two or three hours at a time on walks around the estate or to the cove.

I picked up my knife to cut the meat on my plate, but soon hurried to retract my fingers. Luckily, Mr. Bailey was engaged in conversation. I could only hope he hadn't noticed the state of my nails. Slipping my hands under the table, I slid the nail of my forefinger under the one on my thumb, trying to dislodge the sand there.

Admiral Donovan rose to a stand at the head of the table, and a hush fell over the guests as all eyes turned to him. He waited until there was complete silence before speaking.

"Thank you all for being here," he said, casting his eyes over the group. "It is a pleasure to see friends and neighbors after so many long years and to celebrate with you the end of the war—and our victory."

A bit of soft applause sounded from a few of the people at the table, including Diana.

"Yes, yes," the admiral continued. "I count myself fortunate to have played a part in it." He put a hand on Theo's shoulder beside him, his mouth stretching into a rare smile. "And my son too. *Captain* Theophilus Donovan."

Theo's lips pulled into something between a smile and a modest grimace, but I could see the gratification in his eyes as he looked up at his father.

"At the age of six-and-twenty, no less," his father said. "He will be an admiral before we know it!"

Theo's smile flickered slightly, but he reinforced it, offering a little chuckle as he accepted the praise and congratulations of those nearest him with grateful nods.

The admiral waited a moment for the exchanges to die down,

then raised his glass. "To the end of the war. And to Captain Donovan."

I picked up my glass and smiled as Mr. Bailey touched his glass to mine, making a small *clink* before we raised them to our lips and drank.

We left the men to their port once the meal was over, and I felt a bit of the weight lift from my shoulders as the doors to the dining room shut behind us. Refinement didn't come naturally to me, and I felt that more keenly than ever in the company of so many for whom it did—people who had been raised peeking through the balusters at the guests in their finery below and dreaming of the day when they could join in. I, on the other hand, had spent the greater part of my childhood running in boggy peat fields and churning butter I had helped milk from the tenants' cows.

Two years at Mrs. Westwood's seminary could not undo such a childhood. And truthfully, I didn't want it to. I missed such freedom. My world felt much larger then than it did now, confined as I had been to Blackwick Hall and its environs for so long.

Diana sought me out immediately in the drawing room, along with Emmeline and Amy Crosland. All of us had been at Mrs. Westwood's together, where Diana had taken us under her wings like a mother hen. Among women, beauty was so often the deciding factor in the selection of a ringleader, but while Emmeline was inarguably the fairest of the group, she could not compete with Diana's commanding personality or vast experience. Diana had been formed and educated in the belly of a third-rate ship of the line, and all of us had naturally been awed by her relative wisdom and knowledge of a world that went beyond the confines of Mrs. Westwood's papered walls.

"Well?" Diana said expectantly, her arm threaded through Emmeline's.

I considered pretending ignorance, but I knew precisely what she was asking me. "He is . . . verra agreeable." My accent fluctuated, hovering between the Westwoodian one, as I had dubbed it, and Scottish.

"He seems to share your sentiment," she said with a little raising of a brow.

"*Or*," I said, reverting fully to my natural accent, "he's simply a gentleman who kens how to engage a woman in conversation."

"*Conversation*," Diana repeated in a valiant attempt at mimicking my brogue. She laughed, well aware that she had failed. "Are we Scottish again, then?"

"We?"

She waved a hand. "I could never manage to imitate you. My tongue is simply incapable of it. But Mrs. Westwood would be terribly proud of you tonight. A pity you never displayed your talents while we were still there. I think she quite despaired of you."

I tucked my lips in, feeling a bit of guilt. "'Twas wrong of me to tease her so."

"Oh, but then where would we have had any entertainment?" Emmeline chimed in. "Nothing could make her eyes go quite so wide as an *Och* or some Gaelic from your lips."

I gave a reluctant smile and shook my head. When I had begun at the seminary, it had been close on the heels of my father's death, and I had not appreciated the woman's efforts to cure me of my Scottishness or to wrap me about in the confines of the decorum and behavior expected of all her students. The loss of my father had made me hold tightly to home and heritage, and I had channeled the stubbornness of my grandmother, Elizabeth MacKinnon, who had lived with us until her death when I was thirteen. She had been a firebrand until her death and a woman I had looked up to my whole life. So, when accentuating my brogue or telling tales of changelings and kelpies had entertained the other girls and aggravated Mrs. Westwood, I had been unable to resist.

I had matured enough since then to feel remorse for my behavior, even if the memory still elicited a smile. At the very least, Mrs. Westwood would find educating her other students mere child's play after dealing with me. "Tonight I repent of my conduct. I dinna wish for yer father to censure her for failin' in my education." I straightened, clasping my hands together just below my chest as Mrs. Westwood had always instructed us to do. "I shall be a model graduate of Mrs. Westwood's."

Diana's nose scrunched up. "How very dull."

The door opened, and the Admiral walked in, followed by the rest of the men.

"Diana," he said once his eyes found us. "Play something for us on the pianoforte."

I glanced at her, wondering if she would resist her father's peremptory command, but she smiled and agreed, leaning in toward me. "I must prove to the admiral that I have gained *some* accomplishments while he has been away, or he shall order me back to Mrs. Westwood's."

Looking at me with a little quirk of the brow, she clasped her hands together as mine were and made her way to the piano. The other guests took their seats.

Except Theo. He stood just inside the door, hands clasped behind his back. He looked every bit the captain—handsome, erect, a clear gaze made all the more piercing for his vibrant blue eyes. Would he avoid me whenever possible? Keep me at arm's length for fear I would renew the sentiments expressed in my letter?

Amused at the thought, I looked away, focusing my attention ahead again. Mr. Bailey had found a seat beside Emmeline, making me wonder if I had been correct about his attention to me. He was simply the sort of man to make himself agreeable to everyone and ensure no one was neglected.

I tried not to tense when I noted Theo walking toward me out of the corner of my eye, but it was impossible not to feel on edge. When I had left the letter in his trunk all those years ago, I had imagined the moment when the two of us would be reunited. In my mind, though, the war had lasted only two more years, not seven. And in my mind, I would have been waiting on the dock as he swung over the ship's deck, too impatient to come take me in his arms for the gangway to be let down. Neither had our imagined reunion been accompanied by Diana's singing and playing, accomplished as she was.

I silently reiterated my intention to replace whatever memories of me lingered in his mind with a fresh and overwhelmingly positive impression.

"Elena," he said, speaking quietly enough that he would not interrupt his sister's performance. "Or Miss MacKinnon, rather." His pair of fine eyes surveyed me, and he made a furtive but overly precise bow.

I formed my mouth into a more somber expression and inclined my head with an equal measure of formality. "Captain Donovan." I spoke the way Mrs. Westwood would have approved of, persuading myself it had everything to do with my conversation with Diana a few minutes ago and nothing to do with wanting to impress Theo.

His nose scrunched slightly—an expression he had made frequently as a younger boy. Hardly the reminder I needed when I was valiantly trying to forget the things I had admired about him. Things were different now.

"Just Theo, if you please," he said, stationing himself at my side.

I glanced at Admiral Donovan, who was watching Diana play, pride making his chin lift well above his cravat. "I think your father would regret hearing you ask people to dispense with the title."

He gave a little chuckle, directing his attention toward his father. "No doubt he would. But not with you, surely."

My heart gave a little flutter. It might have been preferable if he *had* treated me with stiff civility. Had he forgotten how he had humiliated me so many years ago? Why the familiarity now? I had often wondered if he thought of me over the years—as the poor young girl, besotted with him—and if he had read my letter aloud to his fellow lieutenants, laughing at my expense in the wardroom.

But there was no trace of condescension in his demeanor now. Neither was it like Theo to laugh maliciously at anyone.

I should have known. He was too upright, too chivalrous to act in any way unbefitting a gentleman. And if he meant to pretend it had never happened, I was more than happy to oblige. He was being merciful, and I could appreciate that.

He glanced at me, his gaze lingering for a moment before he looked away again. "I hardly recognized you at first."

I dropped my hands to my waist, clasping them more tightly there, afraid the sand under my nails might give me away—as though they weren't hidden by my gloves. Would he have had as much difficulty recognizing me if he had seen me slipping into the kitchen fresh from the cove, with sand all over my skirts and hair disheveled, hoping to avoid the carriage that had brought him and his father to Blackwick?

"Am I so changed?" I asked, afraid to hear the answer.

Diana rose from the piano bench and gave a curtsy, and Theo and I both applauded.

He looked over at me as he clapped, giving a nod as his gaze surveyed me once again. "Undeniably."

I gave a polite smile and looked away. That was what I wanted—for him to admire the changes, to regret ignoring me all these years when he saw the woman that overeager young girl had become. And I was fairly certain he *did* admire what he saw.

But how satisfying was it for him to admire the Westwoodian Elena when the true version of me was nowhere near as refined?

Admiral Donovan was in conversation with Emmeline's mother in the seats nearest us at the back, but they suddenly looked around the room, the admiral's gaze settling on Theo and me. It hovered there for a moment, shifting between the two of us.

"Captain Donovan," he finally said. "I was just telling Mrs. Aldridge here about your stint on the *Conquest*. She has a cousin she believes was aboard the very same vessel."

Theo looked at me, a glint of wry humor in his eyes—at his father's chosen form of address, I could only assume. "It is good to see you again, Miss MacKinnon. You look well."

"Just Elena, if you please," I said.

He held my eyes another moment, nodded, then joined his father and Mrs. Aldridge, leaving me to fret over how I had handled things until Mr. Bailey came and claimed my attention.

Chapter Three

When I woke in the morning, the lion's mane had returned, the plait I had arranged it into before bed simply unable to contain it during my tossing and turning. I rang for Hitchen and asked her to see if Tait would be willing to teach her the techniques she had used to smooth my hair last night.

"I prefer havin' someone I ken and trust arrangin' it," I said, trying to lessen the offense I might be giving with my request.

Tait mercifully agreed, taking a quarter of an hour to instruct her, after which Hitchen put her newly learned skills to use. And while my hair was not as neat as it had been last night, it was a far cry more contained than usual, and I made certain to heap my compliments upon Hitchen. In truth, I required very little of her and was far from being an exacting mistress in most things —indeed, I often wondered why I troubled to employ a lady's maid at all. But if my future was to hold more engagements like last night's, I would have no choice but to make better use of her.

Of the Donovan men, only the admiral was present at the breakfast table when Diana and I made our appearance there.

He had a newspaper beside his plate and seemed to be discussing it with Mr. Bailey, though they paused civilly at our entrance.

"Do my brothers intend to take up lazy habits now?" Diana asked as she served herself from the sideboard and I followed after.

The admiral frowned. "Captain Donovan breakfasted early and went out, Phineas is buried in his books, and heaven only knows where Valentine is. Still abed, I imagine."

Diana took a chair and motioned for me to sit in the place between Mr. Bailey and the admiral, with whom I had yet to speak since his return, beyond a brief greeting. This moment seemed particularly unpropitious for interaction, though, and I made no move to disturb his reading. Instead, I readily accepted Mr. Bailey's conversation when it was kindly offered.

However, he was soon obliged to see to the matter of ensuring transportation for his mother's arrival later in the day. As he left the room, Valentine Donovan passed into it.

At first glance, there was little resemblance at all between him and Theo, for Valentine was dark in both eye and hair color. While he was undeniably handsome, he was also undeniably less amiable. That did not seem to prevent him from making any number of connections and conquests amongst the fairer sex. He and Theo both carried themselves with confidence, but Theo's was rooted in his integrity, while Valentine's seemed to be more arrogant. Not that I disliked Valentine. He had never been unkind to me. His manner was simply brusque and his countenance often somewhat saturnine—particularly in the company of his father.

Valentine made quick work of it at the sideboard and took the empty chair next to me, setting to his food as I sipped my tea.

The admiral suddenly folded his newspaper, setting it down beside his empty plate.

I opened my mouth to speak to him, but he rose from his chair, bid us good morning, and was soon gone.

"You mustn't mind the old admiral's poor manners," Valentine said, glancing at the door as it shut behind his father. "He only has so much polite conversation in him, and he expended both yesterday and today's quota praising Theo."

I bit my lip, glancing over at him. It was strange to hear Valentine, of all people, criticizing someone for incivility. He himself could be curt to the point of rudeness at times. But he shot me a quick smile before setting a piece of mutton in his mouth.

It was kind of him to make light of things, even if there *was* a hint—well, a gob, more like—of resentment in the joke, but I couldn't help but wonder how the admiral truly felt toward me. Did he begrudge how long I had trespassed on their kindness? Was I an inconvenience?

As soon as I had word from my brothers, I would need to discuss the matter of returning home to Scotland. Hopefully, that would be done sooner than later.

Chapter Four

In the early afternoon, all those wishing for some time out of doors took to the grounds of Blackwick Hall, after which we planned to enjoy tea and a small nuncheon on the south lawn.

Mr. Bailey and I walked together; he had sought me out, making me again reevaluate my conclusions about him and how he viewed me. Had Diana been correct to surmise that he was eager to marry?

And, just as importantly, how did *I* feel about that? For all my training at Mrs. Westwood's, I'd had little opportunity to display my few accomplishments in the company of gentlemen or, as a consequence, to think seriously about matrimony. Perhaps it was time for that to change.

Change was precisely what I wished for. While Mrs. Donovan had been ill and while Diana needed company at Blackwick, I had at least felt useful. But now? I longed for something new—for freedom. For home, perhaps. But it had been so long since I had been to Scotland, I hardly knew whether to call it home anymore. Just the thought brought me low and made me feel homeless.

"Your home is in Bedfordshire, is it not?" I asked Mr. Bailey as we made our way around the edge of the long pool on the west side of the estate. The fountain trickled musically as the sun reflected off the shimmering water.

He nodded. "Yes, that is right. Have you ever been?"

"No. I regret that my own knowledge of this island is limited to my home in the Highlands, Mrs. Westwood's Seminary, and then Blackwick Hall, of course."

"Ah, but there is something to be said for settling in one place, I think. There is nowhere I would rather be than my home in Bedfordshire. My mother often encourages me to leave it for London or Brighton, but I am happiest at home."

I smiled at him, but my mind was busy considering what it would be like to marry Mr. Bailey and to be obliged to convince him to leave his estate, with not even the sea nearby to indulge my imagination with what wonderful places lay beyond.

A footman hurried up to us, and we came to a halt. "Mr. Bailey, your mother's carriage has just arrived."

"Ah," he said, "thank you." He turned to me, offering an apologetic smile. "If you will excuse me, Miss MacKinnon."

"Of course." I watched for a moment as he made his way toward the front of the estate. I could find no fault with Mr. Bailey. He was handsome, attentive, easy to converse with, and well-connected, which was something Mrs. Westwood had always highly prized. But neither could I find a desire within myself for more than friendship between us.

Perhaps I was expecting too much. I was not fourteen anymore, after all. Friendship was more than many people began marriage with.

"You match."

I whirled around and found Theo beside me. "Pardon?"

He nodded at my dress, an old dress of Diana's, and I looked down at the white muslin I was wearing. A pattern of small, purple flowers was printed across it. I hadn't even noticed their color until now, but the blooming lilac bush beside me brought it out.

Theo went to the bush and leaned his head toward one of the blooms, inhaling. His mouth drew up at the side, and I watched him, wondering what thought must be crossing his mind.

He looked up at me, and his smile grew wider. "It has been some time since I smelled something so sweet and fresh."

"What? No lilac bushes aboard the *Conquest*?"

"Sadly not. It is one thing I miss while at sea—the smell of plants like this one." He let the stock of blooms glide between his fingers, and a few petals floated to the ground.

"How do you feel being back ashore? At home?"

He turned from the lilacs so that we faced one another and, looking at me for a moment, tipped his head to the side. "I haven't decided yet." His glance moved somewhere behind me. "I believe we are making our way to the tent now." He put out an arm. "Walk with me?"

I accepted it with an unnecessary fluttering of the heart, letting him set the pace we adopted, which was slow and leisurely, causing us to fall behind the rest of the group.

"It is strange to be on land again," he said. "They speak of finding your sea legs, but I confess I am finding it difficult to find my land ones again." He planted his next footstep on the grass more firmly than necessary. "Every footstep feels so solid, so . . . final."

I glanced at him, unable to repress a smile. "But this is grass. If you wish for something softer, the only thing you will find is sand."

He laughed. "Where do you think I went this morning? It is strange, I know. But the ground here feels very unforgiving and disconcertingly stable."

I envied him such experience—to know what it felt like to be lulled asleep by the sound and movement of the waves. Blackwick Hall was just far enough from the water that I couldn't hear it from my window. "Walking on the marble floors inside must be agony."

He grinned at me in a way that felt unsettlingly familiar. "Excruciating."

His smile was the part of him least changed—most like the one that had been extended to me on my first visit to Blackwick Hall when I was only nine. Seeing it produced a little twist of nostalgia in my heart. Before Theo had been an idol of sorts for me, he had been my friend. I missed that friendship.

"Your accent is gone," he said after a moment.

I swallowed, my insides squirming.

"I remember being absolutely convinced you were speaking another language when you and your father first came here."

I smiled at the memory. "You couldn't understand a word I said."

"Not at first, no. But it didn't take long."

"Not for you," I said. He had been the first one to begin to understand me. "Diana required you to translate for a week at least."

He glanced over at me, something he had been doing quite often, I noticed. Perhaps he was still in doubt about me, given how different I was since our last meeting.

"You certainly do not require my translation services anymore," he said.

We reached the tent, freeing me of the obligation to respond. My accent had certainly softened over the years, but it was far from gone, and had I been speaking naturally, it was likely I would have had to repeat a thing or two for those unaccustomed to hearing brogue.

The large, white tent provided shade for the two wooden tables brought out by the servants. One was laden with bread, butter, tarts, sweetmeats, and an offering of lemonade, which was already poured in small, crystal glasses. The other was laid with a tablecloth and surrounded by chairs.

Theo retrieved a glass for me, and I noted Admiral Donovan's eyes on us, his expression impassive but fixed.

"Miss MacKinnon."

I turned. Mr. Bailey slowed as he approached, his mother on his arm. Her piercing gaze was settled on me, making me wonder what her son must have told her for her to regard me in such an acute way. She was a regal sort of woman, with the sort of bearing Mrs. Westwood would have applauded. In fact, they reminded me of one another a bit.

Lady Bailey's tight-lipped expression was a stark contrast to the genial one her son wore. I resisted the impulse to put a hand to my hair, which had undoubtedly grown more disordered during our time outside. Hitchen had been obliged to use far more pins than Tait to achieve what she wanted, and they hung heavily on my head.

"Mother, allow me to introduce you to Miss MacKinnon and Captain Donovan." Mr. Bailey gestured to his mother. "This is my mother, Lady Bailey."

"A pleasure to meet you, Lady Bailey." I executed the sort of curtsy I had been forced to practice again and again, lowering my eyes demurely, while Theo gave a courteous bow at my side.

Lady Bailey let out a strange, trilling laugh. "Ah! What a relief! When my son told me you hailed from Scotland, I was afraid I would be incapable of understanding you."

My eyes shot involuntarily to Theo, and my hand tightened around my glass of lemonade.

"It is a rare thing indeed when I can understand a Scotsman," she continued as Admiral Donovan approached. "Just last week, I spoke with one at a dinner party—or rather he spoke *at me*, for I could not understand a word he was saying! How delighted I am to see you again, Admiral."

They exchanged greetings, and I tried to keep the smile plastered on my face as we all moved to take the seats set at the empty table.

Lady Bailey continued as the admiral pulled out a chair for her. "I imagine you and Captain Donovan must find it easier to understand them than it is for me. Sometimes it seems as though the world is being overtaken by Scottish soldiers and officers."

My lips were beginning to fight my insistence on their cooperation, and I tried to relax my hold on my glass, which tightened with every word from the woman.

"For my part," Theo said, "I would gladly take on more Scottish sailors. His Majesty's Army has never been so robust, I am sure you will agree, and it is thanks in no small part to the presence of strong and diligent soldiers like Miss MacKinnon's brothers." He glanced at me. I felt my throat tighten in response to his defense of my family and my country. "One need only look to Lord Cochrane to see what a greater presence of Scotsmen in the Navy might achieve for us."

Lady Bailey's nostrils had begun to flare above her tight smile, but at this, she let out another laugh. "The disgraced Cochrane? Hardly a man to hold up as a standard."

Tension charged the air around us at the mention of the scandal that had gripped the nation two years ago—the prominent Scottish captain and politician expelled from the Navy amidst allegations of fraud—and I glanced at Mr. Bailey to see what he made of this exchange. He was frowning, lips shut tightly, with no apparent intention of opening them to intervene.

"Lord Cochrane is an upstanding gentleman," Admiral Donovan replied tersely. "His reelection proves unequivocally how he is regarded by those who know him."

"How strange." Theo interjected, sitting forward in his seat and peering into his glass of lemonade. "The liquid lies so still. I am accustomed to my drinks mimicking the sea. A tempest in a teapot, one might say."

The conversation turned to discussion of life aboard sailing vessels, and I shot Theo a look of gratitude, which was met by a hint of an understanding smile.

Lady Bailey proved to be a force to be reckoned with, however. She was adept at ruffling feathers and bringing controversial topics to the fore of any conversation. She seemed particularly interested in asking questions of me and making comments that sounded complimentary but were laced with disdain for Scotland and its people. I was apparently exempt from such judgments, for she seemed to have set me in a class all my own—a welcome exception to the unfortunate rule my barbaric countrymen followed.

And while they had disagreed on the topic of Lord Cochrane, the admiral and Lady Bailey found themselves in harmony on one subject at least.

"There has been a host of midshipmen and lieutenants turning merchant since the war ended," the admiral said with unveiled disdain.

"You would rather they starved on half-pay, I take it?" Valentine said.

I watched the admiral with wide eyes, waiting for the inevitable retort that always accompanied interactions between him and his second son.

Lady Bailey gave a forced shudder. "To think of sacrificing the honor of serving the King for . . . for *money*."

"Said by someone who has never felt its lack," Valentine said in a snarling under voice.

I couldn't help but agree with him. There might be honor serving King and country, but I knew enough of my own brothers' struggles to find a way to support themselves to sympathize with anyone who made the sort of decision the admiral alluded to. Now, in particular, when there were so few positions for an abundance of sailors, difficult and practical decisions had to be made.

By the time Lady Bailey left to settle into her bedchamber and rest before dinner, I was on edge and feeling restless after so much time constraining myself into a Westwoodian mold. It was suffocating.

Rather than making my way inside and giving Hitchen the time required for helping me prepare for dinner, I slipped away from the tents unnoticed and made my way toward the path that led down the cliffs and onto the beach.

The wind that so often whipped about the tall, white cliffs, pulled at my bonnet, and I hurried to remove it, tugging at the pins to release my hair as I made my way past the large rock the waves licked up against.

Rocks, sticks, and shells littered the sand, and I picked up a handful, taking them with me to the small sea cave at the other end of the beach. Theo and Valentine had shown me this cove on my first visit to Blackwick Hall, and we had spent as much time as we could playing there. When I had returned after my father's death years later, it had been the first place I had sought out—and the one I had come to after slipping the letter into Theo's chest. I had adopted it as a refuge of sorts over the years.

The large rock that sat at its entrance acted as a buffer against the strongest of the waves. Holding up my skirts with the hand containing the shells, I slipped past the rock and into the space behind, where the cave ceiling dropped low, forcing me to crouch.

"Och," I cried, my hand flying to my head. I slid my hand along my hair to pull it free of the rough rock it had caught on and looked up at the ceiling spitefully. I never seemed to be able to avoid its claws, even after all these years.

I rubbed at the spot that was still smarting and slipped the items I had collected onto the pile I had made between two rocks, listening for the familiar clicking as they made contact and tumbled into place.

On the other side of the assortment was a stretch of smooth sand, dimly lit by the light that managed to penetrate to the back of the cave, and atop it, a scattered collection of tiny houses, constructed of shells, sticks, rocks, and moss. I stared at them, letting my gaze flit from one to the next. It had taken me two weeks to construct these six little houses. They would be ruined by the tide at some point, but only the highest of tides—infrequent as they were—managed to sweep through this part of the cave. Sometimes it merely scattered the materials about, while other times, there was not a trace left of what I had built.

It was strange, this pastime of mine. I had no doubt of that—or at least that it would be regarded so by others. After all, what proper young lady engaged in such child's play? And that was, indeed, how it had begun. Theo and Valentine had been enraptured by the Scottish legends I had told them—of the fae, the kelpies, the brownies. The kelpies and water wraiths more than anything, though, had frightened them, for I had told them that both haunted the sea, and both Theo and Valentine were mad for the Navy.

They had been eager to learn how to gain the favor of the brownies, who might protect them from such dangers, and together, we had made two crude houses as an offering.

I smiled at the memory of how determined the boys had been to check on the houses and reconstruct them when the tide had taken them. For them, no doubt such memories had faded, but not for me. This place had fulfilled two needs of mine: a connection to home and a way to expend nervous energy as I worked with my hands in a way that needlework simply couldn't fulfill.

I held up my skirts and picked my way through the rocks and out of the cave, looking out over the sea. I had often watched for ships in the distance, envying those sailing their freedom, wondering how it would feel to stand on the deck and look out over the never-ending expanse where sea met sky, where there were no bounds, where even the most faraway lands were within reach, where one could fall asleep in England and wake in France.

The freedom the sea offered was unfathomable to me, restricted as I was to Blackwick Hall and its immediate surroundings. And never had that felt so small as it did now, full of people who thought me more like them than I truly was.

Chapter Five

The rain kept us all indoors the next day. I was not one to be deterred by such a thing, but it was pounding rain, and I resigned myself to a long day cooped up inside. It was for the best, perhaps, for I was certain that, if the admiral had wind of my frequent and solitary expeditions to the cove, he would be less than pleased. Certainly, Lady Bailey would not approve.

Mr. Bailey was kind as ever, and I could only assume he had acquired such a trait from his father, for I could find no authentic trace of it in his mother. She laughed often enough, but it was not the type that sought company and mutual enjoyment; it was more like a weapon.

Midmorning, the Baileys received word that the friends they intended to visit had a case of scarlatina in the home. The admiral insisted they remain at Blackwick Hall until it was safe to continue their journey, and I resigned myself to continuing my ruse for some time to come.

When the opportunity allowed for it, though, I made my way to the Orient Room. At least, that was what *I* called it, for its appeal lay as much in the artifacts scattered throughout it as in the books that adorned the high shelves.

I hurried past the study, where the admiral and Theo had retired not long ago. The muffled tones that managed to find their way past the shut door let me know that whatever discussion was happening within was not a happy one. I did not envy Theo such an interaction, whatever the subject.

I slipped into the library and hurried to shut the door behind me, trusting Lady Bailey was not the sort of woman to take refuge in a dusty room like this one. The room was particularly dim today, given the gloomy skies outside, and I went over to the window seat I most often occupied, where I had a view of the sea. It was barely visible today, shrouded in gray mists.

I didn't feel quite so confined when I was in the Orient Room. Whether between the pages of the books, looking out at the sea, or touching one of the relics Admiral Donovan had acquired in his decades of travel, I could almost imagine myself in another land, another world. And today, I was anxious to be in another world.

My eyes had been seeking out Theo far more often than I liked. Had I not managed to leave such a habit behind? And what was I to make of the fact that his own gaze was often directed at me too? I wanted the friendship that was beginning to redevelop between us, but I simultaneously felt the need to punish him for the hurt he had caused me.

But that was the rub. Whether I liked it or not, Theo reminded me of my childhood and of all the things that came along with it—of the hurt I had experienced at his hands, of the mortifying decision I had made with him as the impetus, and, perhaps most uncomfortably, of the days before it had occurred to me to change who I was or how I spoke to please someone else.

Pulling my eyes away from the dreary outdoors, I spotted the model of a ship that sat on one of the bookshelves. It was one of the ships the admiral had commanded years ago, and I had inspected every inch of it, trying to picture what it would be like to live on such a vessel, vulnerable to the elements. I had envied my brothers and Diana's the adventures that lay before them, even as the greatest excitement the two of us had to look forward to now was deciding what color of thread to use on our samplers.

I went over to the long table that displayed the majority of objects that had caught my interest over the years: a jade elephant, a faded scroll, a few small porcelain vases with vibrant blue enamel, and a handful of books. I had seen *chinoiserie* before coming to Blackwick, but these things were different, and they made the attempts to copy them seem unsophisticated and lacking. It was ironic for the admiral to feel so strongly about sailors leaving the Navy to work on merchant vessels when he had acquired all of this during his time working on just such a ship.

I touched a finger to the jade elephant, tracing the smoothly carved lines that ran from tail to tusk, wondering that such a creature should exist in the world and feeling regretful that I should never live to see one.

Behind me, the door opened with a loud creak.

"Och!" I startled, and the elephant tipped onto its side with a *clang* that made me wince. Letting out a curse in Gaelic, I hurried to set it back upright, then whirled around with a shaky breath of relief at the sight of Theo.

He gave me a quizzical look, and I put a hand to my chest to calm my heart, hoping the sound of the elephant falling had masked my unladylike utterances.

"Forgive me, I thought you were . . ."

"My father?" he supplied.

I tucked my lips in, unwilling to admit to something that might betray the way I regarded the admiral.

Theo came up beside me and took the elephant in his hands. "Don't worry. I won't tell him you tried to kill poor Algernon."

A laugh broke through my lips unbidden, and I turned back to the figurine. "I forgot we had named him."

He set it back down. "Oh, yes."

I glanced at him from the corner of my eye. If he remembered Algernon the elephant, there was no chance he didn't remember something more recent like my letter. Unless it had truly meant so little to him....

"Do you think your father knows how often we played in here that summer?" I asked, pushing the unhelpful and irrelevant thoughts aside.

He chuckled. "No. Decidedly I do not. He is not the type of man to stay silent on such a subject."

"Are there subjects on which he *does* stay silent?" I regretted my words immediately, but the amused smile Theo displayed rewarded me in a way that made me feel fourteen again. "Forgive me. I should not have said such a thing. Your father's strength of feeling is undoubtedly what makes him such an effective commander."

His brows furrowed as he picked up one of the books on the table. "No doubt." There was a dry quality to his words that left me surveying him in hopes of better understanding what was behind the response. How *did* he view his father? Theo had served under his command until becoming a lieutenant, and I had seen his father's influence on him firsthand when he had returned to Blackwick before receiving his commission—and my letter. He had been more rigid, as though he still considered himself under his father's orders and liable to be reprimanded at any moment.

His mouth pulled up at the corner. "You had Valentine and me convinced that you could read this." He held up the open book in his hands, looking at me with amusement.

I looked at the jumble of strokes that meant nothing more to me now than they had years ago, and I pulled my lips between my teeth. I recognized the language now as Canton and the book as Sun Tzu's military treatise, but I had insisted to them that it was Gaelic. "When did you discover the truth?"

He flipped through more of the pages. "Not until my father insisted upon reading together—him with this and me with that." He nodded at the other book on the table, *L'Art de la guerre*. It was a translation of the Canton book into French. The Art of War, Admiral Donovan called it.

He laughed, setting down the book and looking at me again. "It took me nearly half an hour to realize that I had been hoodwinked."

"I was desperate for you to admire me for *something*." I inhaled softly, again regretting my words, for they were the exact reminder I didn't wish to provide him—of how I had viewed him then, and what it had driven me to do. I wanted to pretend it had never happened so that we could simply be friends.

His eyes were on me, and I reached for the book. "Your father has it memorized, does he not?"

"Yes. Perhaps not verbatim, but certainly he knows the principles perfectly."

"Diana does, too, I think," I replied.

"All of us do—or did at one time. It was the stuff of dinner conversations in our family, you know."

"Your mother said something similar." I ran a finger along the gold engravings on the front of the book, a reminder of how much of the world I had not seen, how much I didn't understand but wished to.

"She did?" Theo's voice was soft.

I could not help but notice the sadness that had come into his eyes as he looked at me, as though hungry for more about his mother. I nodded. "She and I came here often together—before she was confined to her bed, you know. She would sit over there"—I indicated the red velvet-upholstered *chaise-longue* —"and tell me about the different objects and their stories. The ones she knew about, at least." I looked around at all the books surrounding us. "She loved this room as much as I do."

"You were here, then? During her illness and . . ."

I nodded once.

"I didn't know."

I managed a small smile. I was well aware that he didn't know of my continued presence here or that I had spent a year keeping his mother company, acting as her scribe, and reading to her. Diana had been excellent at ensuring that her mother's every comfort was seen to, but her personality was such that she could not sit still in the sickroom. She needed to *fix* things, and so often what Mrs. Donovan had needed was someone to simply sit beside her. A calmer presence.

"She particularly loved that." I pointed to the ship on the bookshelf.

Theo turned to follow where I was pointing, and his brow furrowed as they fixed upon the model. He walked over, gently taking it from its place.

"The *Dominance*," he said. "This was the one we were all aboard together."

I clasped my hands behind my back, watching him as he looked over it, that same frown wrinkling his brow and making me wish to know what he was thinking.

"She spent a great deal of that time in bed," he said, pointing to the miniature area where the captain's quarters were. "Too ill to do anything else." His frown deepened.

Mrs. Donovan had become sick while aboard the *Dominance* and had never recovered, weakening her until another sickness took her away for good.

"Is it a true model?" I asked.

"Very," he said, taking the few steps over to me. "At least to my memory, it is." He pointed to a place near the bow. "That was my favorite place to stand on a fine day. My mother would come with me there when she was feeling well. Valentine loved it too—back when he loved sailing. Phineas rarely came on deck. He preferred to keep below."

"Reading?"

Theo smiled. "Whenever he could manage it, yes. He would sometimes sneak just *here*"—he pointed to a corner next to a set of stairs, almost too small to see. "My father had little patience for it, I'm afraid, even when Phin was reading books about navigation or what have you. He insisted that there was no book that could compare with experience."

I glanced up at him, feeling flustered at how close we were. "Not even *L'Art de la guerre?*"

He laughed. "That was an exception, but Phin could only read it so many times until my father refused to believe he hadn't memorized it already."

I looked at the hiding place, wondering how Phineas could prefer the pages of a book about sailing to the actual experience of it. I had read a great number of the books in this very library about far-off lands and peoples, but I would trade them in a second if given the chance to see everything for myself.

But Phineas and I were different that way, and he must have felt as constricted aboard the *Dominance* as I did here.

"And what of Diana?" I asked.

Theo chuckled and shook his head. "Diana was to be found anywhere and everywhere, following Father around, teasing the shipboys, falling in love with a lieutenant once, but most often telling the midshipmen how to do their work."

"How delightful." I grinned as I imagined her traipsing about the ship. "She has not changed a bit, then."

"No, she hasn't. At least, not like you have."

My gaze whipped to him. His eyes held mine, a strange look in them that made me feel vulnerable for how little I understood it. Was he admiring the changes he had observed? That was little comfort for a woman pretending to be far more polished and genteel than I was.

"And like you?" I said, eager to shift the focus from myself.

He frowned. "Have I changed? I had not thought it, but perhaps I have. It seems only reasonable. It has been a long time since we last saw one another."

I swallowed at the reference to the time I wanted expunged from everyone's memories. "You are not so very changed," I said.

He directed his gaze at me, a glint of curiosity in his eyes.

"Taller, of course. Blonder." I looked to his square jaw. "More confident, I think." His eyes were a more piercing blue than ever, too, reminding me of looking out over the cliffs and onto the shallowest parts of the water as the sun streamed through it. They were settled on me now, fixed and searching.

I blinked. This exercise was not conducive to my goals. "Fatter, perhaps."

He burst into laughter and put a hand to his stomach, which was entirely flat and devoid of an excess of anything—unless it was perhaps muscle. I couldn't see it, of course, but I could imagine.

"Must be all those ships biscuits." His eyes twinkled at me like the sun glinting on the sea. They calmed a bit, and his smile softened. "I did admire you, you know."

My heart flip flopped, but I contained it. He hadn't admired me enough to respond to my letter. I wanted to say just that as I held his gaze, to understand how he could say such a thing and act as though nothing had happened between us, as though he hadn't dealt me a blow that had taken my wounded pride and heart years to recover from. In fact, I wasn't even certain I *had* recovered from it. Not fully. It had made me doubt myself and question myself in a way that was not easily undone.

The door opened suddenly, and we both looked toward it, where the admiral stood, staring at us with a furrowed brow as his eyes flicked down to the ship Theo still held. I shifted subtly to the side, putting more distance between myself and Theo.

The admiral always wore a somber expression, but I had never been able to persuade myself that it wasn't because he was displeased with me for some reason or another. Now I was unchaperoned in a room with his son.

"Mr. Bailey is looking for you, Miss MacKinnon," he finally said.

I couldn't keep from glancing at Theo. His expression darkened, and he turned away, setting the model back in its place.

"He and his mother wish to take a walk to visit our greenhouse," the admiral continued. "I told them you might be able to accompany them."

I quickly nodded, too eager to appease him to worry over the fact that I was agreeing to spend the next hour in Lady Bailey's company. It would be better to be insulted by her than to spend more time with Theo. Old habits were difficult to cure, and I had certainly made a habit of admiring Theo Donovan from a young age.

Chapter Six

To my surprise, our time at the greenhouse passed pleasantly. Lady Bailey took an interest in the different plants being cultivated there. Diana had very particular ideas about such things after what she had been exposed to during her family's travels and had ensured there was a variety here at Blackwick. Mr. Bailey was, as ever, both attentive and in a good humor.

I could find no fault with him, still. Indeed, the only fault to be found lay within myself. Was I expecting to be swept off my feet? To feel the intense admiration and longing I had felt as a fourteen-year-old girl?

I had grown beyond that, surely. I had the future to consider, particularly if it meant anything for the Baileys to desire my company, and mine alone, on this outing. What if Mr. Bailey wished to see me again? What if he asked for my hand in marriage at some point? Could I set aside the naive wish to feel something more for him and look at it in a purely rational way? I did not wish to be beholden to my brothers for the rest of my life, after all. I had a respectable fortune of my own, but that was not enough to offer me the sort of security marriage provided.

And I *did* yearn for something more. And I couldn't help but blame Theo for that. Or perhaps it was myself I should blame, for it was I who had put him on a pedestal from such a young age, who had opened my heart to him with such reckless abandon that I suspected it was still susceptible to his charms.

As for Lady Bailey, aside from her frequent questions, she seemed to approve of me well enough. The approval was of little comfort to me, though, for it was a veneer that would be stripped away the moment I let down my guard.

When we separated for Lady Bailey's afternoon repose, I accompanied them inside only to make my way back to the door. I needed a bit of rejuvenation for the evening's obligations, and I hoped the cove would provide it to me as it had done yesterday.

It was getting easier to speak in my Westwoodian accent, but every evening while she helped me undress and ready for bed, Hitchen was witness to an explosion of Scottishness, as though it had been building up all day and required an outlet.

The next day, Valentine and Phineas were predictably absent from the expedition, and Lady Bailey seemed determined to encourage her son and Emmeline to walk together. Apparently our time at the greenhouse had not gone as well as I had thought.

The wind had died to a strong and consistent breeze that tugged at my bonnet and the curls peeping from it. Our group started our trek along the long drive that led away from Blackwick Hall, the leaves of the beech trees rustling musically above us. Diana, Theo, and I walked together behind Admiral Donovan and Lady Bailey, who trailed her son and Emmeline.

"It looks as though you have been displaced for the moment," Diana said in a low voice, sending me an amused glance. "No doubt Emmeline shall say something of which she disapproves, and you will take your place again as the preferred match for her son."

I resisted the urge to glance at Theo, whose eyes were on me, and forced a chuckle. "More likely *you* will be next."

She scrunched up her nose. "No. I am far too outspoken for someone like Lady Bailey. I should give her an apoplexy within a se'ennight." She looked over at me. "You *do* like Mr. Bailey, do you not?"

I fumbled over my words for a moment, wishing Diana had chosen a different moment for this particular discussion. I should have been *glad* for it, for what could inspire Theo with more regret over discounting me in the past than hearing about the admiration of other men?

And yet, I recognized the anxiousness I felt for what it was: reluctance to make him think my feelings were engaged or my heart set upon Mr. Bailey. Neither, though, did I wish him to think that I was pining after him. In the confusion of the moment, I failed to commit to anything more than a bumbling, "He is . . . very kind."

Diana laughed. "Very well. I shan't tease you about him today. I will simply *observe*. Speaking of which, have you lost your wonderful accent entirely? Or do you intend to keep it hidden indefinitely? I cannot say I blame you, really, for Lady Bailey seems to have no great opinion of Scotland, but you cannot mean to hide it from her forever. And there is no need for pretending in front of Theo and me."

My cheeks flamed with heat, and I glanced at Theo, whose brows were furrowed, his questioning gaze upon me. I couldn't even decide which part of Diana's guileless speech I should address. Should I deny that a match between Mr. Bailey and myself was the goal of my deception? Should I try to defend myself against the deception entirely? I *had* no real defense, and I could see no way forward but to embrace the truth, uncomfortable as it was.

I glanced toward the Baileys, who had adopted a quicker pace and put a fair amount of distance between us as we neared the village. "I find it awkward to make the shift back at this point. And too difficult to explain it." I resisted the urge to look at Theo—to see what he thought of the situation.

"Devilishly difficult." Diana's glance flew toward her father with an expression half-stricken, half-laughing. She was not accustomed to guarding her tongue in front of me, but now that her father was home, things would be different. Seeming satisfied he had not heard her, though, she continued. "I hope you will inform me beforehand if you *do* intend to slip into your lovely Scottish, for I should dearly like to be there to see Lady Bailey's face." The group before us had reached the beginning of the village, and they turned around to face us, putting an end to our conversation.

I was left to settle for myself whether to continue speaking in my Westwoodian manner with the knowledge that Theo was now aware it was a farce. If I continued it, he was bound to think ill of me, for not only was it dishonest—a character flaw someone like him could never condone—but he would be left to assume that I did it in an effort to make myself agreeable to Lady Bailey and her son. But the alternative was to answer any manner of uncomfortable questions from the admiral and the Baileys, and that was no more palatable.

I chose to keep my Westwoodian speech, for the damage was already done with Theo. If I did choose to revert to my natural accent in front of the Baileys, I would do so at a more auspicious moment. Assuming such a thing existed.

Chapter Seven

By the time we returned to Blackwick Hall two hours later, both my composure and my hair had been ruffled past help. No matter how much I attempted to convince myself otherwise, I *did* care what Theo thought of me, and I was beginning to care less and less what Lady Bailey thought, for she was impossible to please. Neither could I deceive her forever, as Diana had pointed out.

And yet, somehow, I could not bring myself to face the repercussions of changing my speech. I was left feeling agitated and resentful, though whether I resented Lady Bailey's high expectations or my own surrendering to them, it was difficult to say.

The group passed through the front door and, rather than following them inside, I made my way to my place of refuge. I untied my bonnet strings as I passed out of view of the house, then pulled the hat from my head.

Holding up my skirts, I shuffled down the path that led from the cliffs to the cove. The tide was reaching its lowest point, but the damp, smooth sand that preceded it revealed how high it had been hours ago. Had it been high enough to annihilate my creations?

Pulling a deep breath of the briny air, slipped past the rock and into the cave's entrance. The fairy village was untouched, and I let out a little sigh of relief. For some reason, finding it had been razed would have put me out more than usual today.

A breezy draft blew into the cave, pressing a few of the many pins that littered my hair into my head. I hurried out of the cave where the wind was less forceful and put my fingers to the most aggravating spot, itching it as best I could without disrupting the coiffure. It was no use, though. My ringlets had turned into the awkward waves and kinks natural to my hair.

I let out a breath of aggravation, setting down my bonnet on the nearest rock and pulling out the pin protruding into the crown of my head. Once it was out, I shut my eyes, reveling in the relief that followed its removal. I began plucking more pins, setting them inside my bonnet as hair fell to my shoulders and over my forehead. I needed a respite from playing the English lady. My hair would be a mess when I returned to Blackwick, but I could twist it into a knot and hide it beneath my bonnet before leaving the cove to avoid alarming the servants on my way in. Simple enough.

The breeze tugged at the fallen hair, and I brushed it away from my face, turning so that the wind worked in my favor.

I stilled. Theo was just stepping from the path onto the beach, devoid of his tailcoat, which allowed his sleeves to ripple in the breeze. He chuckled at the sight of me. "It appears we had the same idea."

Using both hands, I whipped my hair back behind my head, trying to twist it to give it the appearance of still being coiffed, for I could hear Mrs. Westwood's voice in my head.

A woman's hair inevitably reflects her character, be it loose or precise.

If Mrs. Westwood could see me now, it would be immediately apparent to her that I was every bit as unkempt and disheveled outside as I was inside, for not even my best attempts at the proper accent could compensate for the state of my mane, kicked up as it was with every whisper of wind. And perhaps she was right, for my hair seemed as eager to explore the world around as I was. More of her maxims came to mind.

A man's baser instincts are never mobilized with greater rapidity than at the sight of a woman's hair undone.

Loose hair cannot but lead to loose conduct.

Upon reflection, Mrs. Westwood had been unusually preoccupied with hair. And besides, I knew Theo too well to believe him so little master of himself.

But I should still leave. *That*, at least, I had learned from Mrs. Westwood.

A woman's reputation is delicate, prone to shatter into a thousand pieces at the mere whisper of the clandestine.

And another.

Nothing is more sure to become public than the meeting that an unmarried man and woman believe to be private.

Could I think of nothing else besides her ridiculous sayings?

"I was just leaving." I hurried to pick up my bonnet. The twenty pins it was holding spilled onto the sand, and Theo hurried over to help me gather them.

"You still come here sometimes, then?"

I glanced up at him as I set three more sandy pins into the bonnet. "Yes," I said. "More than sometimes of late."

His brows went up. "How often is *more than sometimes?*"

Both of us made to grasp the last few pins scattered on the sand between us, and, just before colliding, our hands hovered in midair.

Our eyes met, and both of us smiled as I reached for the pins and dropped them with the others. "Before preparing myself for dinner each day."

"So often?"

We stood, and I brushed the sand from my skirts before pushing my hair behind my back. There was no managing it at this point. I lifted my shoulders and grimaced. "After living here with only Diana for so long, I fear I have become very unused to company and find it somewhat tiresome."

"Should I leave, then?" He gestured behind him to the path he had just come on.

"No, no," I hurried to say. "It is not your company I find tiresome."

His lips turned up at the corner, and his eyes softened. "I am glad to know that."

Those eyes might well be the death of me. Did Mrs. Westwood have no truisms about avoiding looking into a pair of exquisitely blue eyes? Not that it mattered, for I was not obeying the ones she *had* taught me. Imagine what she would think to know I was violating two of her maxims at once. I had never been a very good student, though, had I? She no doubt expected this sort of behavior from me.

Theo took in a breath and turned toward the sea. "I like your idea of coming here. Perhaps I shall steal it. I, too, am woefully unaccustomed to being in company so often and find it exhausting."

"Oh." I smiled and turned away toward the path, making as if to leave.

My wrist was grasped, and with an explosion of thudding in my chest, I turned back toward Theo.

Our gazes met, and my smile faltered at the unexpected gesture. He dropped my wrist. "Don't go." That same hint of a smile appeared. "It is not your company I find tiresome."

I laughed lightly. "You have spent years on a ship with a host of sailors. How could you possibly be unaccustomed to being in company?"

He smiled wryly. "You might be surprised how lonely the lot of a captain can be."

I held his gaze, wishing I better understood him. I had read his mother dozens of his letters, but he was still a mystery—

perhaps more than ever, for I couldn't understand his conduct toward me.

"Your new accent persists, I see."

I looked down at the bonnet in my hands, tilting it so that the pins inside it shifted. It was true. I hadn't reverted to my natural speech, despite Diana betraying my sham. There was little purpose in pretending I was an exemplary student of Mrs. Westwood's, and while I knew a fear of how he might react to hear me speak, it was unreasonable to put off the inevitable any longer. "I reckon it seems strange to ye," I said, embracing my Scottish lilt, "my pretendin'."

"There it is," he said with a smile. "Strange? No. But my curiosity is piqued. What made you do such a thing?"

I reached a hand to the pins and rubbed two of them together, trying to think how to explain the choice I had made. I shrugged. "Sometimes 'tis simply easier to blend in—to meet expectations."

The lines in his brow furrowed ever so slightly. "I understand that. I admit that I was a bit disappointed when I first spoke to you to find your accent had been lost entirely."

I blinked. "Disappointed?"

He nodded.

"Why?" I found it difficult to conceive of such a thing. My accent had always been conspicuous evidence of how I differed from those around me here in England.

He lifted a shoulder. "It is how I remember you." His eyes surveyed me, and I tried to stay still, resisting the urge to squirm at the memory such a phrase might be bringing to the forefront of his mind. "And you were never meant to blend in, Elena."

I turned, and my hand stole to my hair, further evidence that I did not conform to what an English lady should be. I had never minded my hair until I had begun at Mrs. Westwood's and seen how different it was from the other girls' tame coiffures.

Theo's admission that he had been disappointed about my lack of Scottish accent was a relief, at least. It was nice to speak normally again.

He gestured to the smallest of the sea stacks on the beach. It was more of a boulder, really, six feet long and three feet tall at the highest point. "I see the *Alba* is still here."

My hair was quickly forgotten as I smiled at the memories his words conjured—Theo, Valentine, Diana, and myself atop the boulder, pretending to be sailing for France, thrilling as each wave crashed against it and sprinkled us liberally with seawater. I had chosen the name for it—*Alba*, the Gaelic word for Scotland.

With a gentle tweak of the head, Theo invited me to join him in walking toward it.

"Perhaps it has been waiting for a captain who can manage it," I said.

We reached the rock just as a wave lapped up against the edge nearest the water, and he put a hand to the stone, running it along the surface. "You overestimate my abilities if you believe me to be such a captain."

"Perhaps Diana will take it on."

He laughed. "She always insisted upon that role, didn't she?" He pushed his sleeves up to the elbows and bent to pick up a rock at his foot, rubbing it between his fingers as he straightened. It was long, dark, and smooth, and he suddenly bent low, cocked his hand back, and thrust it toward the water. It passed the smallest waves breaking on shore and skipped across the water.

I watched, counting each skip until it disappeared into a gathering wave.

"Eight," I said.

"I counted nine." He looked at me through narrowed eyes.

"Eight," I repeated.

His brows rose, and he bent to pick up another rock, handing it to me. "You think you can do better?"

I held his gaze and accepted the rock in my free hand without saying a word. My brothers and I had skipped hundreds of rocks on the loch near Benleith. It had been ages since I had made the attempt, but I had been quite good back then. I fiddled with the rock until I found a position that felt natural in my fingers.

Theo watched me with amusement, arms folded across his chest, but I fixed my eyes on the water as I drew my arm back, keeping my hand as level as possible. I thrust it forward and flicked my wrist so that the rock went sailing into the air.

It buried itself in the first wave it reached.

Theo covered his mouth with a hand, but the pinching around his eyes and the subtle shaking of his shoulders left no room for guesswork. He was laughing at me.

I tucked my lips in. "I am out of practice."

He nodded, clearing his throat and trying for a serious expression. "Of course."

"And 'tis much easier to skip a rock on a loch than over large waves."

"Large?" he said, dropping his hand.

"Well, large compared to the ones on the lochs, I mean."

His eyes narrowed as he looked at me, a glint of humor still there. "I suppose I shall have to take your word for your skill."

I smiled, determined that I would practice whenever I came to the cove now. "What brought *you* here? Couldna bear walkin' on the hard lawn any longer?"

His eyes twinkled appreciatively at me, and he picked up a small shell fragment from the sand, looking out to the waves. "A need to be near the water, I suppose."

"Ye miss it?"

His eyes went to me. "Yes." Mouth turning down at the

sides, he looked to the shell in his hand and let it drop into his palm. "I *am* glad to be home, to see everyone, but . . ."

"The sea must feel more like home to ye than Blackwick by now."

He nodded. "I think I have become too used to being my own master, too, which I am decidedly *not* at Blackwick."

I sent him a commiserating smile. Perhaps Theo was less content in his father's company than I had assumed.

The wind kicked up again, sending my hair up and around, pieces fluttering against my cheeks and into my eyes. It would be an unmanageable knot, and Hitchen would soon be obliged to force it into some arrangement suitable for dinner and the evening's activities.

"I should go now." I tried to pull it all back into one hand while keeping the pins from spilling again.

Theo watched me for a moment, and I couldn't help but think of Mrs. Westwood's maxims and what this encounter at the cove would have been like if my hair had as much power over Theo as she had insisted it would. Part of me wished that it had. But perhaps my hair was too wild to have any effect.

"Here." He took the bonnet from me, allowing me use of both hands.

"Thank you," I said, sheepish that the focus should be on my disorderly hair. Whatever image of a proper English lady I had hoped to convey to Theo, today had managed to undo the better part of it. Fingers flying, I separated the hair into three sections, mercilessly snapping the tangled hairs that resisted my efforts, and weaving the section into a plait that reached to the middle of my ribs.

He took the pins and handed me my bonnet, which I slipped over my head with an attempt at a smile.

His eyes were pensive and observant, and it made my heart race and my cheeks warm, for I couldn't at all tell what thoughts lay behind them.

He dropped the pins into my hand. "Perhaps I shall see you here tomorrow."

My heart sprang to life as I met his eyes. He wanted to be friends. That was all. He needed a place to satiate his longing for the sea, and this was the best place for that, accessible as it was.

"Perhaps so," I said.

Gripping the pins in my hand, I turned and made my way back to the path, entirely uncertain whether I should return the next day or not.

Chapter Eight

It took twenty minutes for Hitchen to brush through my hair, and I apologized to her profusely, promising that the next time I went to the cove, I would do so with my hair covered or at least plaited.

I felt refreshed if somewhat restless after my time with Theo, and when the group of us gathered before dinner, I couldn't help wondering if he would choose to sit near me. However, Mr. Bailey claimed that honor—his attentions were becoming more marked, it seemed to me—while Theo sat between Emmeline Aldridge and her mother, who had come again for dinner. They lived but a mile from Blackwick and had been some of Diana's and my only visitors over the past two years.

I refused to pay any heed to the little flare of jealousy ignited by the sight of Emmeline and Theo and instead turned all my attention to conversing with Mr. Bailey. We had spent a great deal of time together over the past few days, yet somehow I felt I knew him but little—or him me. What would he make of my time with Theo at the cove? Or the fact that I went there at all? I had no doubt whatsoever that his mother would regard it in the same way Mrs. Westwood would. Unchaperoned? Hair uncoiffed? She would need smelling salts.

When the men rejoined us in the drawing room, I was surprised to find the admiral approaching me. "Miss MacKinnon, we have had little chance to speak since my return. I must apologize."

"Not at all," I hurried to say. "I understand you have been occupied with naval matters as well as seeing to your guests."

"Yes, there continues to be a great deal of work to tie things up now that the war is over. I have no doubt Diana meant well when she planned the dinner the other night, but the timing was unfortunate. It would have been better to have waited a month or two when I could devote my full attention to matters here."

I looked to Diana, who had instructed two tables be set up for games of whist and was looking through the decks of cards, most of which had been stored away and unused for years now. She spoke with the group of people congregated around her as she sorted the cards in front of her. It was very like her to assume everyone had her same energy, to wish for no time to be wasted before celebrating her brother and father's return.

"I hope it is not too much of an inconvenience," I said. "You have shown the utmost generosity allowing me to stay here all this time, and I wish for you to know how much I appreciate it, Admiral."

He waved an impatient hand. "I did not refer to your presence here. I am glad to have been able to provide a home for you, naturally. You are my goddaughter, after all, and I flatter myself your father would be pleased with things. It was what he wanted, you know—for you to receive a proper education and make a fine match."

My gaze involuntarily went to Theo, who was standing near one of the windows with Valentine.

"He would make a fine husband."

My eyes widened as my head whirled around. But the admiral was not looking at Theo—naturally. His eyes were fixed on Mr. Bailey, who sat across from Diana and had begun assisting her with the cards.

"Many of our hopes are pinned on that family," he continued, keeping his voice low. "I would like to see *you* settled, of course, and then Captain Donovan has an ambition to be positioned on a ship again, but there are precious few placements for captains now, you know, so Admiral Bailey's influence at the Admiralty is vital." He turned to look at me and offered one of his stiff smiles. "In any case, seeing his son settled is bound to make him more amenable."

I tried to return a smile but only managed a faltering one. Was he saying that Theo's future prospects depended upon my ability to persuade Mr. Bailey into offering for me? And then my accepting him?

Diana hurried over to me and took me by the hand. "Excuse us, Father, but I must steal Elena away for a game of whist. She and Mr. Bailey will be playing against Phineas and me, and I have sworn to win."

"Go on, then," said the admiral, giving me a subtle but speaking smile that made my stomach roil.

I had not played whist in years, and Diana and Phineas beat Mr. Bailey and me handily. Phineas was particularly adept at cards, and playing brought out a more gregarious side of him than I had ever seen.

Mr. Bailey and I gave way for the winning team's new challengers, Theo and Emmeline. The admiral, Lady Bailey, and Mrs. Aldridge were seated on the sofa nearest the table, casually watching the play, while Valentine leaned against the wall between two windows, sipping leisurely from a glass of brandy.

Lady Bailey asked her son to retrieve her shawl—despite the fact that there were two chairs before the fire if she cared to move—and, not feeling particularly enthusiastic about sitting with her, I joined Valentine. He was an enigma to me in many ways, and if I had not known him when he was younger, I might have been hesitant to approach him, for he could look quite unsociable.

"Routed, were you?" he asked.

I clasped my hands before me and rested my back against the wall beside him. "Decidedly. Shall you play?"

His crooked smile made an appearance. "I prefer higher stakes—and games that are not played in pairs. I like having full control over the outcome."

I frowned. "But one never has *full* control even then, surely, for a great deal depends upon the hand one is dealt."

He looked over at me over the top of his glass, the same smile still there. "That sounds like an excuse for losing."

I laughed. "Yes, and a great comfort to me. But *someone* must lose, so it may as well be me." I was no match for Diana's competitiveness.

"You are more generous than I." He sipped the last of his brandy, casting his gaze at the whist table.

I surveyed his profile for a moment, wondering what had turned him cynical. He had not always been thus. "Who do you think will win this rubber?"

His eyes narrowed slightly as he looked over the four players. "There is no telling—not with Theo and Di playing. They have always been the most ambitious in the family. With the admiral watching, though, my money is on Theo."

When Diana called her father *the admiral*, it was done teasingly, but not with Valentine. There was an ironic bite to the words.

"Because he plays more carefully when your father watches?" I asked, too curious not to prod.

"Because Theo needs more than anything to please him. I am not even certain he realizes there is another option."

Theo deliberated over his cards, his brow furrowed in concentration, making him look more like his father than usual.

"I have tried to show him another way," Valentine continued, tipping his glass sideways so that the last drops trailed to the other side, "setting the bar low enough that, no matter what he does, he will never be the admiral's *greatest* disappointment, but" —he grimaced and lifted his shoulders—"I am afraid it is too ingrained in him at this point. The admiral's aspirations and Theo's are one and the same." His countenance grew darker, more troubled. "Perhaps I have only made things worse for Theo, though, for now all hopes are pinned on him. I imagine the admiral will simply refuse to die until Theo is Lord of the Fleet."

I didn't respond, my mind full of his words and my eyes trained on Theo. I had seen what Valentine spoke of—Theo's ambition, the way he looked when he received praise from his father, as though there was nothing greater in all the world. I had seen, too, his father's influence over him during his short spell home all those years ago. So much of Theo's playfulness had disappeared during that time.

Mr. Bailey returned with his mother's shawl, wrapping it about her shoulders with care and concern. She was fortunate to have such an attentive son. He looked up suddenly, and our eyes caught. He smiled, and I returned it.

Valentine cleared his throat, and I glanced at him, wondering if he meant something by it.

"I gather you are to be the lamb sacrificed on the throne of Theo's career advancement?" He nodded at Mr. Bailey, who flattened a ripple in the shawl.

I blinked and turned my head away, unsure how to respond to such a remark. Valentine had a way of saying the things no one else would say.

"Did your father say that?" I asked.

"I overheard some of your conversation earlier. If it is what you wish, then by all means . . . But if not, you mustn't submit or feel obligated, Elena, whatever the admiral has said to you." His gaze moved to his father, hardening slightly. "He can't help but think of everyone around him as sailors under his command, pawns to move about the board, and if you comply with his wishes rather than your own, you will end up like Theo."

"What do you mean *like Theo*?"

He set down his glass on the windowsill and looked over at me, his dark eyes fixing on mine in their peculiarly unnerving way. "Chasing someone else's dream, for that is what Theo has been doing, whether he realizes it or not."

"He loves sailing."

"He does. And he is an excellent sailor. He likes it on its own merits, unlike my father, who is hungry for advancement and recognition. But Theo is bound to lose his love in the pursuit of what my father wants for him."

I thought of Theo's words about how lonely the lot of a captain could be.

Valentine's jaw shifted from side to side as he watched his father. "He will continue to steer Theo away from anything that does not advance his career—including having a family of his own, for he sees my mother as having impeded his own progress."

I looked over at him, sick at the picture he painted. Was this simply his cynicism rearing its head?

Yet he met my gaze clearly. "It is true, awful as it sounds. It is why he has grown so strict about the presence of women aboard the ships in his fleet."

Mr. Bailey had finished seeing to his mother, and he came over to the window. Valentine shortly excused himself, leaving me to wonder what to do with all he had said.

Chapter Nine

Despite my best judgement, I did return to the cove the next day. I needed it—the fresh air, the conversation, the respite from Lady Bailey, the friendship. It had been so long since I'd had the friendship.

I'd had Diana, of course, to keep me company. But there was something different about Theo. Diana was always so confident, so fast-paced, so unapologetic in her opinions. And Theo . . . he had a softness, a deliberateness about him that I found as refreshing as the salty air I anticipated with my walk to the beach. In fact, he reminded me of his mother, and I missed my relationship with her.

I had so many questions after speaking with Valentine, too, and I hoped perhaps more time with Theo might help me understand him better. Did he know of his father's wishes for me and Mr. Bailey?

Before stepping onto the trail that descended in a winding path, I stopped atop the cliffs, looking down at the part of the cove visible from above. My hair was plaited, as I had promised Hitchen it would be, but I had left my bonnet behind after a look at the trees and how the wind moved the leaves. It would have been tugging on my bonnet mercilessly now as I peered down to the stretch of sand and rocks below, and I hated that feeling.

Theo was nowhere in sight as I searched the beach. Had he reconsidered coming? The thought pulled my stomach tight, but perhaps he was right to stay away. Mrs. Westwood, at least, would approve. I walked down to the beach, intent not to allow myself any disappointment when it became clear he was not there. I had survived enough disappointment from him to last me a lifetime, after all.

I checked on my houses—all still intact but for one, likely a victim of the wind—and used two seashells from the pile to reconstruct it. I went still as a thought occurred to me. I had left Theo at the beach yesterday. What if he had come to the cave and seen my strange creations? He would certainly know they were mine, for they were so much like the ones we had made as children, and I had admitted to him that I came here often. Even if he had, no doubt he would simply regard it as one of my many peculiarities.

I sighed.

I took a few of the smoother rocks from the hoard of supplies I had amassed in the past few weeks and made my way out of the cave, determined to improve my skill. The first skipped but once—an improvement, surely, but I was resolute that I should be able to skip it ten times.

Concentrating on the waves, I waited for one to crest and crash before throwing the second rock.

One. Two. Three. Four.

"Three. Well done."

I whipped around, and a smiling Theo clapped as he came up to me. Like me, he wore no hat, and the sight of his blond hair being tousled by the wind had my heart in knots.

He put a hesitant hand toward the few rocks I still held in my palm, his eyes asking me permission.

"I counted four." I allowed him to take one. I spoke naturally again, and it felt like a weight from my shoulders. Here, at least, I could be myself. As if I needed any more reasons to crave my time at the cove.

He leaned toward me, blue eyes dancing. "I did too."

I smiled at him. "But four isna eight."

"Nine," he said. "But no, it is not. But you said yourself you are out of practice, and I have the distinct advantage of having skipped more than my share of rocks over the last few years." With a flick of the wrist, he sent a tiny rock flying forward. It skipped seven times.

"I envy yer experience."

He had stooped over to pick up another rock, but he glanced at me. "What? Skipping rocks?"

"Nay. Well, aye." I lifted my shoulders. "All of it. I've never even *been* on a boat, to say nothin' of sailin' across a sea or an ocean."

His eyes searched mine. "And that is something you would like to do?"

"Ye think it strange?"

He blinked. "No, it is just . . ." He frowned and turned the rock over in his hand, rubbing the sand from its surfaces. "Perhaps Bailey can provide such an experience for you." He threw the rock, and it disappeared into the waves as mine had done yesterday.

My heart twinged at his words—at the implication within them that I would marry Mr. Bailey and that he was the best person to give me the experience I wished for.

"Bailey is a good man," he said. "A good choice."

I stared at him, my teeth clenching. "Is that so?"

He looked at me, and his jaw worked for a moment before his gaze returned to the sea. "Yes." He threw another rock. This one, too, quickly disappeared. The water was becoming more rough.

I let out a small, caustic laugh. Perhaps Valentine's cynicism was contagious, or perhaps to blame was the hurt I felt at hearing Theo talk so easily about my future with another man, but anger bubbled up inside me all the same.

"A good choice because his father's more likely to grant ye a captaincy if I *do* marry him?"

His eyebrows snapped together. "What?"

My nostrils flared as I met his gaze.

"What did you say?" he repeated.

I had never seen him look so stern, and I turned away, scooping up two rocks and a great deal of sand with them. "Ye wish for another ship to captain, and Admiral Bailey has the influence to grant it to ye." I brushed the sand away from the rocks, and the grains fell onto my skirts.

Theo was still turned toward me, and the tenseness in his body made me feel disquiet, as though I had crossed a line. "That may be, but"—he rubbed his lips with a hand, his brows knitting more tightly than ever—"what does that have to do with you and his son?"

My confidence gave way to more and more doubt. He looked so very foreboding, his eyes reflecting the turbulent, gray waters so that I could hardly see the blue in them. "Yer father said the match would please Admiral Bailey, which would make him more amenable ta . . . helpin' ye."

His jaw tightened, and he turned away.

"Is that not true? Do ye not wish to command a ship?"

He pushed his sleeves farther up his forearms. "I . . . I do." His frown deepened again. "But even so, I would never want to be given it as a result of *that*. If the Admiralty gives me command, it must be on my own merits, Elena. I cannot believe you would think—" He stopped, his jaw tightening as he looked away.

I swallowed the lump in my throat, feeling stricken and suddenly unsure of myself. Whatever hope I'd had of coming to a better understanding of Theo today was quickly disintegrating. He was as obscure as ever.

"I've made ye angry," I said. I hated the thought.

He shook his head. "I merely did not know you thought so little of me." He threw another rock, and it skipped twice before being swallowed.

"Nay, I . . ." I took a step forward, hand stretched toward him, then checked myself. My hand dropped, clenching at my side. "I *dinna* think little of ye. Far from it."

He searched my face for a moment, then let out a breath that made his cheeks puff up with air.

"Forgive me," I said.

"There is nothing to forgive, Elena." He held my eyes until I nodded.

We continued skipping rocks in silence, and his brow grew more and more pensive and less frowning as the silence lengthened, punctuated only by the breaking of the waves, the sounds of two gulls circling overhead, and the small splash of our rocks on the water. I stole a glance at him every now and then, wishing for a glimpse into his mind.

He said he did not wish for my marriage to Mr. Bailey for the sake of his own career. Why, then, did he say Mr. Bailey was a good choice? Why did he push me to him with such words? He wished for the match for *some* reason, it seemed. The thought stirred uneasily in my stomach.

I knew not what to make of his behavior toward me or the way he looked at me sometimes. But perhaps the desires of my adolescence had not left me entirely and made me see things that weren't there. If Valentine was right and Theo was as determined to advance in the Navy as his father was, he would not be searching for a wife. Neither would he be telling his desired wife that Mr. Bailey was a good choice.

For all I knew, Theo may never wish to wed. The admiral had evidently regarded Mrs. Donovan as a hindrance, an inconvenience. Had he influenced Theo to think in such a way too?

"What of you?" I asked, trying to keep my voice light and detached. "Now that ye're home, shall ye marry?"

"No." The response was immediate, and it lodged somewhere in my chest, making it feel tight. "I am not sure that I ever shall." He said the words in a flat, emotionless tone.

My heart dropped into the pit of the stomach. I had been right. Theo had never looked on me with anything more than friendship. My letter, the time I had spent dwelling upon the thought of us together—it all hung upon my shoulders with an unbearable and shameful weight at his words.

"I should be goin' inside," I said, forcing myself to smile as he met my gaze.

The strong breeze played with his hair, making me want to run my fingers through the gold and caramel tresses. I looked away, tucking my own escaping hair behind my ear and turning to leave.

"Elena, wait."

I stopped and turned just enough to look back at him, waiting.

His eyes were full of whatever had made him stop me. "Have I angered you?"

I shook my head. I was not angry. I was hurt. I was falling for Theo Donovan every bit as quickly and even more deeply than I had when I was fourteen, and he would break my heart again.

"Nay. I'm not angry."

He looked as though he wasn't sure whether he believed me. He put out a hand. "Friends, then?"

I swallowed. *Could* I be friends with Theo? I was beginning to sincerely doubt that.

But I couldn't say no. Not with the way he was looking at me.

I stepped forward and took his offered hand, which sent a

pulse through me that was much more than friendly. "Aye. Of course."

He smiled, but there was a wry quality to it—sad, even. "Tomorrow, then?"

I gave a nod, but I wasn't certain I would come. As much as I might wish to spend each afternoon with Theo here at the cove, I wasn't naive enough to think it would lead to anything but heartache for me.

Chapter Ten

The men went riding the next morning, and I was grateful for it, as it spared me the necessity of choosing how to spend my time—and with whom. We women passed our time in the drawing room at the pianoforte, perusing periodicals, and seeing to whatever needlework had been neglected.

The amount of proper conversation such a day required nearly had me pleading the headache. But I knew Diana wasn't particularly fond of Lady Bailey, and it would be too bad of me to leave her to entertain the woman.

By the time the men returned from their riding and people retired to rest and dress for the evening, I was spent and wanting nothing more than the fresh air and freedom at the cove. I had told Theo I would be there too. But to what end?

I paced the length of my room a number of times, my hair unpinned, waiting to be either plaited for the cove or arranged for the evening. I glanced at the window and stopped abruptly, noting with a lurching heart the figure of Theo, coatless and hatless, walking away from Blackwick Hall and toward the cove.

I put a fist to my lips, bouncing it thoughtfully against my mouth as I considered my options. It felt cruel—not to mention distinctly contrary to the wishes of my heart—to leave him there waiting for me. But wouldn't going there be cruel to myself? I could go and explain to him why I could not continue meeting him there, but to do so would be to admit to him for the second time what I felt for him, and I was not at all certain my pride or heart could bear to be rebuffed another time, particularly after the way he had pushed me toward Mr. Bailey yesterday.

I yanked the curtain closed, concealing the window's view, and hurried over to pull the bell that would bring Hitchen to help me dress for dinner before I could change my mind.

Theo's eyes were on me, a searching look there, as we all entered the dining room, but he did not approach me as I had feared he might. Perhaps he understood the message I had sent with my absence at the cove, for he stayed away from me all evening, spending the majority of his time with Valentine. The distance made my heart twinge and ache, but whenever I felt impelled to seek him out, I forced myself to remember the days I had spent waiting for his response to my letter and the disappointment that had grown each time there was nothing.

I noted, too, a degree of strain between Theo and his father over the course of the night, and I hoped it had nothing to do with what I had said to Theo yesterday about a marriage between myself and Mr. Bailey helping his advancement. The last thing I wanted was to cause conflict in the Donovan home.

I purposely partook of a late breakfast the following day, knowing that Theo was one to both rise and eat early. I could not continue avoiding him indefinitely, but a bit of distance while I decided upon the best course for the future was merited. I needed to put him out of my heart and mind, a task made all but impossible because I could not avoid him entirely.

In the late morning, we went out to the lawn to enjoy a game of battledore and shuttlecock, with the admiral and Lady Bailey looking on. Mr. Bailey and I played together on the far side of the lawn, while Theo, Diana, and Emmeline played on the other end.

It was impossible to be preoccupied while engaged in such an activity, and I enjoyed myself more than I had in some time. I far preferred exercise outdoors to yesterday's proper activities inside.

"You are a skilled player, Miss MacKinnon," said Mr. Bailey as he hit the bird toward me.

"As are you," I said politely, shuffling to return it to him with my own battledore.

He reached to receive it, missing it by a few inches, and the bird fell to the ground. "I fear my skill is quite eclipsed in this regard." He picked it up and gave it a little whack.

It sailed to my left, and I hurried to follow it, reaching out my battledore just enough to prevent the bird from falling.

"I have never met a woman so able at the game," he said.

I looked over to Diana and Emmeline, who reached simultaneously for the bird Theo had hit toward them and both missed. Emmeline doubled over in laughter while Diana picked up the bird and determinedly hit it toward her brother. Theo's chest rose and fell quickly with his breath, and I wondered how long he and I would be able to keep the game going if we were to play together.

But we were not playing together. I was with Mr. Bailey, and I should be using my time with him to come to know him better. Perhaps I would feel a desire for more than mere friendship once I understood him better.

"Did you not wish to follow your father into the Navy?" I adjusted the feathers on the bird, then whacked it toward him.

He hit it back, keeping his eye on it as he responded. "No. I have always stayed with my mother—she dislikes sailing and believes ships to be a man's domain, you know—and I think it has led me to become too accustomed to the comforts of life on land."

The bird sailed back and forth between us, and I tried to count as I listened to him.

Thirteen. Fourteen.

"I am a creature of comfort, I fear," he continued. "I have only been aboard a ship two or three times, and it did not agree with me."

Fifteen. Sixteen.

"In what way?" I asked.

His expression became thoughtful. "It is so very unpredictable—one never knows whether the day will be calm or tempestuous. I like firm ground under my feet—as does my stomach."

Nineteen. Twenty.

I smiled politely as I hit back, but his words left me feeling discouraged. I had never been aboard a real ship to know how well it would agree with my stomach, but I was fairly certain it would not affect me in the way it affected some. I had a strong constitution—the result, I imagined, of a childhood full of adventure. I had had more than enough firm ground and predictable days in the past seven years, too, and I itched for something different, to see new places, to have my courage tested.

"I prefer to be at my home, I suppose," he said. "I hope you shall see it someday—my home, I mean. I am sure you will appreciate it."

"I am certain it is lovely. Thirty-six," I said breathlessly when the bird finally dropped to the ground.

"Have you finished?" Diana called out to us. "Emmeline and I have aggravated Theo with our ineptitude, I am afraid, and I suspect he will begin aiming for my face if he is not supplied with a better teammate. Would you care to play with him, Mr. Bailey?"

"Certainly," he said as we approached the others. "Though, if he wishes for the best player, it is Miss MacKinnon rather than myself who should play with him."

My gaze went to Theo and his to me, and I suddenly felt unprepared to face him. Would he ask me about my absence from the cove yesterday? What would I say? What *could* I say?

Theo pulled his eyes from me. "I am sure you are being modest, Bailey. Come, let us make the attempt. Certainly you and I can do better than what Di, Miss Aldridge, and I managed."

Though I should have felt relief, his words stung. Was he angry with me? Or had he seen the dismay in my eyes?

"Yes, and the three of *us* can enjoy the refreshments before they are gone." Diana set down her battledore and linked one arm through mine and one through Emmeline's.

I allowed myself to be pulled in the direction of Lady Bailey and the admiral. I could have sworn the latter looked at me with more sternness than was usual, but why? I had been doing just as he wanted, hadn't I? Playing with Mr. Bailey. Perhaps I was imagining the displeasure once again, though.

The three of us continued to the small table with bread and cold cuts behind the chairs. My eyes were inevitably drawn to the two men playing at shuttlecock as I picked up a roll and set it beside the meat and cheese on my plate.

"Theo is out of sorts today." Diana had come up beside me and was looking at the men with her head cocked to the side.

I forced my gaze away from him and down to my plate. "Is he?"

She nodded. "Decidedly. He was much less patient than usual, wasn't he, Emmeline? I think it is owing to my mother."

My brows knit, and I looked at Diana. "Your mother?"

She nodded. "I suspect it is more difficult than he had anticipated to be here without her. I have seen him go into her bedchamber more than once. He was always her favorite, you know."

"Di," I said chidingly.

"Oh, you know it is true." There was no resentment in her gaze, only the simple frankness she so often wore. She looked back to Theo. "I think he cannot forgive himself for being gone when she died."

My gaze rested on him, watching but not truly seeing the quick movements as he played. My mind was focused on the conversations I had had with Mrs. Donovan about her children —on the letters I had written on her behalf to Theo and on the record I had helped her keep. In the tumult of Theo's return, I had forgotten about the journal entirely. But if his conscience was smarting over his absence during her illness and death, if he regretted missing his mother's final days, I was in a position to provide a bit of salve to such a wound.

Surely, I could do at least that much for the man.

Chapter Eleven

I watched from my window later on, looking for any sign of Theo on the path to the cove, but I looked in vain.

He was quieter than usual at dinner, more distracted and somber when addressed, and when we retreated to the drawing room, he again kept company with Valentine.

I took an early breakfast in my room the next morning, hoping that I might retrieve the journal for Theo while others were dining. Once I was dressed and my hair coiffed, I made my way down the quiet corridor toward Mrs. Donovan's bedchamber. I had spent a great deal of time here during her illness, and even the feel of the engraved door handle brought back a rush of memories that caught in my throat.

I cleared it away and pushed the door open enough to see inside, stilling at the sight of Theo sitting on the bed. I hurried to pull the door closed again, wincing at the way it squeaked.

"Elena?"

I shut my eyes, the air suspended in my lungs. After what Diana had said yesterday, I should have thought that perhaps *this* was where Theo came after breakfast each morning. I had assumed he had seen to correspondence or perhaps gone for a ride—or a walk to the cove, even.

Taking in a quick breath, I pushed the door open again and faced him.

He was standing beside the bed now, gaze fixed on the doorway where I stood.

"I didna mean to disturb ye," I said. I glanced down the corridor, realizing I had spoken in my normal accent. But there was no one there.

"Not at all," he said, walking toward me slowly. "Did you need me?"

Did I need him? What a question. "Nay. That is . . . I came to retrieve somethin' for ye."

His brows went up. "For me? In here?" His eyes looked pinker than usual, making the blue stand out all the more brightly. Had he been crying?

I was torn between the impulse to leave him in privacy and the desire to provide some relief to him. "Yes," I said, settling for the truth. "I can return later, though."

He shook his head and gestured for me to enter. "Come in."

I nodded and turned, hesitating over whether to close the door. I settled for leaving it ajar—a compromise for Mrs. Westwood. Though, now that I thought of it, she hated compromise.

Not for all the rubies in the world would a genteel woman compromise her reputation.

Evidently, I was not a genteel woman. Neither did I know what I would do with all the rubies in the world even if I had been.

Theo was looking at me curiously, and little wonder.

I walked over to the bedside table, crouching down and opening the cupboard in the bottom. There was a tall, leather book within. I pulled it out, setting it atop the table as Theo slowly made his way over, watching me.

"I should have thought to tell you of this sooner." I wiped

my hands down my dress. This room still felt saturated with emotion, even two years since Mrs. Donovan's death.

"What is it?" He came up beside me and picked up the leather book, letting it rest on his arm as it fell open.

The corner of my mouth drew up. "The ship's log."

He glanced up, his bright eyes resting on me.

"That was what we took to calling it, at least. I gather your mother would sometimes help your father with it aboard the *Dominance*. She was in the habit of keeping records when she returned home, as I am sure you know. When she became too ill to continue them, I managed to convince her that those of you who were unable to spend her last days with her would find such a thing valuable. It's a record of her days and the things she found important." My hands grasped at the fabric of my dress, a nervous gesture I couldn't resist as I thought of his father's reaction when I had shown the book to him. When the admiral had returned from his wife's burial, I had informed him its existence. He had flipped through the pages with a cursory glance and thanked me. And then he had left the book in this room.

Theo's chin quivered slightly, and his throat bobbed behind his cravat as he quickly dropped his eyes to the paper. His head moved slightly as his eyes traveled over the page.

I hesitated, wondering if I should leave.

He looked up at me, his brows furrowed in an unmistakable frown. "*You* wrote this for her?"

I nodded, unsure what to make of his reaction. "I think dictating helped pass the time. The days could be long for her. She could do so little once she was confined to the bed."

His eyes were still fixed on me, making me feel suddenly warm.

Finally, they dropped back down to the book. "It was you, then."

I waited, unsure what he meant. He hadn't known of the

existence of the ship's log until just now, so he couldn't be referring to it.

He looked up. "You who wrote the letters. I recognize the handwriting." He held up the book slightly, which was open to two pages full of my own script.

"Yes," I said. No doubt it seemed strange to him that it should have been me rather than his own sister who had done such a thing. Was he bothered by it? My hands fiddled in front of me. "Diana would have done it, no doubt, but—"

He shook his head. "I knew it was not Diana, but I thought perhaps it was a companion my father had employed. Diana can barely stand to sit still for five minutes, let alone write the sort of letters Mother sent me. I believe Diana wrote me two letters in the last five or six years."

I laughed, feeling relieved that he seemed not to be annoyed. "She has always hated correspondence."

He grimaced. "I worried more than once that she would be plaguing Mother rather than helping her."

My mouth twisted to the side. "It is true that she is not very well-suited for the sickroom."

He chuckled. "An understatement if I ever heard one. You know that when I was once ill on the *Dominance*—this was early on, before I had accustomed myself to storms and such—it was her idea to put me in one of the midshipmen's cots and rock me to and fro, as though the motion of the ship wasn't already enough."

I covered my smile with a hand. It seemed very much like Diana to try to make something better only to make it worse.

Theo seemed to enjoy my attempt to cover my amusement, and his eyes regained some of their lively twinkle as he looked at me. He took in a breath and dropped his gaze to the book again.

"This is a treasure, Elena. As are the letters you transcribed." He glanced at me as he turned the page. "I kept them all and often reread them, for they brought me great comfort. I received so few letters over the years that they were a bright spot in what was often a very dark time."

I swallowed, thinking of one specific letter and the fact that he hadn't bothered to respond to it, despite all the letters he had sent his mother—letters I had read to her in this very room. They had made it all the more difficult not to admire him—for his valiance, for his love for his mother—and to feel my own humiliation all the more intensely.

"She would be glad to know that," I said softly. "Your letters did the same for her, I know. One of the last things she requested was to have the most recent one read to her again." My voice caught at the memory of the tender hours before she had breathed her final breath, and Theo looked at me, expression full of sympathy.

"She loved you from the beginning," he said.

I tried to swallow down the lump in my throat. Diana and I had not often spoken of Mrs. Donovan since her death. Diana's way of grieving, I had found, was to avoid the topic.

I smiled wanly. "I gave her no choice in the matter. I was determined she should, for I admired and loved her greatly. I hardly knew my own mother."

He reached for my hand, taking it in his and pressing it. "I am so grateful to you for being here for her until the end. For being here when I was not." His frown returned, deepening more than ever. He shook his head, and his nostrils flared as his nose grew pink. "She should never have been aboard the *Dominance*. It was no place for a woman."

He dropped my hand, and my heart plummeted along with it.

"You asked me the other day if I intend to marry, and I told you I may never do so. My mother is the reason." Looking down at the ship's log, he shook his head. "I shan't make the same mistake as my father, subjecting a wife to the harshness of the sea. No woman should have to bear such a life. I could never ask her to."

I clenched the hand he had held, hiding it behind my back. "Perhaps you simply haven't met the woman who will make you see things differently."

His gaze flew to mine, and I felt my emotions fraying. I tried for a smile, knowing it failed dismally, and turned to leave.

"Elena, wait."

I stopped but kept still, for my eyes had already filled to the brim, and I refused to let Theo see me coming unhinged.

"I regret if my father ever made you feel any sort of obligation at all with . . . with Bailey."

I blinked hurriedly, and a tear escaped. I couldn't brush it away without betraying myself, so I let it slide down my cheek.

"I have spoken with him on the subject and made things quite clear," Theo continued.

My stomach clenched. So that *was* the cause of strain between him and his father, and I had not imagined the gravity in the admiral's expression yesterday.

"Bailey *is* a good choice," he said more softly. "But not because of anything having to do with me."

My throat thickened all the more, and I suddenly wondered if perhaps Theo had done me a favor by simply not responding to my letter all those years ago. The pain of a forthright rejection like this one was acute.

I gave a nod and left the room.

Chapter Twelve

I hurried down the corridor, intent that, if Theo had any thought of coming after me, I should be gone by the time he did. I took the servant staircase upstairs, having no interest in coming upon anyone. The way my tears left a streak of cold down my face told me that my cheeks were red and hot to the touch. My chin quivered with my attempts to trample the emotion that insisted on making itself evident in my face.

I looked down the corridor when I reached the top to ensure I would not be seen on my way to my bedchamber. Fortunately, it was empty, and I took refuge behind the closed door of my equally empty room, where I hurried to sit on the bed.

I swiped the tears from my cheeks, determined that there should be no more of them. I would not be undone by Theo yet again.

Perhaps he was right. Mr. Bailey *was* a good choice. I had yet to find anything consequential to say against him. He was kind. He was intelligent, a gentleman who took care for my comfort. And while his mother was not a woman I imagined I could ever look upon as I had looked upon Mrs. Donovan, Mr. Bailey at least did not seem to harbor the same prejudices she did against my people.

He deserved that I should give him a real chance, without any hidden reservations based on some silly hope of something developing between me and Theo. It was time I put the past where it belonged and looked to the future, for I could not remain at Blackwick Hall forever—neither did I wish to. Marriage would afford me a freedom I hadn't known since coming to England, and Mr. Bailey was not the type of man to be overly strict in his expectations of me.

I would not do it for Theo's naval career. I would do it because it was rational, and it had been a great many years since I had been rational when it came to Theo Donovan.

That changed now.

I took in a deep breath and released it slowly, along with any thought of Theo and myself as anything more than friends.

Letting go felt strangely liberating. I could breathe again now that the weight of such an unlikely hope was removed from my shoulders.

That evening, I was good for my word. I set my full concentration on Mr. Bailey whenever we were in company, not allowing myself even a glance in Theo's direction. I harbored him no ill will. It was simply good-natured indifference.

Mr. Bailey was attentive, as ever, and apart from the time the men lingered over their port and we women went to the drawing room, he hardly left my side all evening, leaving little room for doubt about his intentions.

When he went to refill my tea, Diana hurried over to me, nudging me with her arm and leaning in to whisper in my ear.

"You would not have left me in the dark if he had discussed marriage with you, would you?"

My cheeks warmed. "Of course not. There has been no discussion . . . no mention of . . ." I trailed off awkwardly as the image of Mr. Bailey making such an offer presented itself to my mind. Would he expect a kiss afterward? My gaze followed him as he made a remark to the admiral while pouring from the teapot. It was strange to think of kissing him, perhaps because I had never thought of doing so with anyone but—

"Well," Diana said, "given how inseparable the two of you have been all evening—as if none of the rest of us even *existed*, I confess my surprise. But I am glad for it, you know, because now I am not obliged to be angry with you for keeping such a secret from me."

Mr. Bailey returned with my cup, and Diana smiled widely at him before gliding away, shooting me a saucy look as she did so.

The only thing to mar an otherwise pleasant evening was the knowledge of the obstacle before me: how to go about ending my ruse. It was terribly awkward, and I sincerely regretted my foolish decision to adopt it in the first place.

But that was a decision already made, and now I had to face the consequences. Did I shift my accent subtly, making it more pronounced one day at a time in the hopes that the change would be gradual enough they wouldn't notice? Did I confess the whole truth to Mr. Bailey, hope he would not be angry, and trust he would manage to smooth things over with his mother? Did I continue speaking my Westwoodian English, hoping that my Scottish brogue would surrender to it in time, making my ruse into a reality?

I fell asleep well into the night to such a conundrum, and I was no closer to solving the problem when I woke, feeling anything but rested. Reluctant to go down to breakfast without having made a decision, I ordered Hitchen to have it brought to me in bed.

My appetite was small, and I picked at my toast and sipped sporadically at the tea in my cup as I considered my dilemma. The question at hand was how much of the past—*my* past—I was ready and willing to leave behind in the interest of the future. I had been in England now for seven years. At what point would I accept that I was becoming more and more English and less and less Scottish?

I had made the decision to abandon my history with Theo, and it had been liberating. Who was to say that I would not feel the same way about all the other things I had been holding onto?

Suddenly feeling overwhelmed with fatigue and indecision, I put my tray aside and slumped back down onto my pillow, shutting my eyes, and before long, I fell into another restless slumber.

I dreamed myself at the cove, building a fairy house amongst the others, taking care that the shells and sticks were all in their proper place. I heard my name called, and I turned to see Mr. Bailey and his mother walking toward me on the beach. I hurried over to them to prevent them from seeing the houses, certain that it would be the end to everything if they did.

Mr. Bailey took me by the hands and, without any preface, offered marriage right then and there. I hesitated for a moment as he stared at me expectantly, finally saying, "Yes."

He took me in his arms and kissed me ruthlessly as I struggled to break free. When I managed to free myself, I ran away and toward the cave, where Mrs. Bailey stood with a bucket, emptying the never-ending supply of water onto the houses, which washed away, leaving no trace behind.

I woke with my covers in a tangled mess, the result of my thrashing, I could only assume. Taking in a deep, shuddering breath, I waited for my body to realize that it had been nothing but a dream. Such silly imaginations were simply the result of me suddenly facing a new future I had yet to become accustomed to, but the dream left me feeling shaken, all the same.

I summoned Hitchen to help me, pulling out one of my older dresses—a worn, tan one with half-sleeves. I needed to go to the cove to see the houses and assure myself they were still intact. I knew if they were not, Lady Bailey would have had nothing to do with it, but it seemed of paramount importance despite that.

Perhaps the sea air would clear my head, too, and that was something I needed if marriage was truly to be considered.

Chapter Thirteen

My boots lay behind me in the sand just beyond the tide line, where they would be protected from any rogue waves. I stepped into the water, taking in a sharp breath as the cold surf ran over my feet, my ankles, then wetted the hem of my dress. I would certainly not be wearing it to dinner, and it was a relief to wear something that allowed me to move as I wished to.

I had known a small fear Theo might be here, but I had heard him and his father speaking in raised voices in the study on my way out. It seemed to be a more and more frequent occurrence these days.

I breathed in deeply, searching the horizon. Was I willing to forgo this sort of thing? Lady Bailey would not approve. She would be the new Mrs. Westwood in my life if I married her son. That was a lowering reflection if there ever was one.

But she was not here right now. This was my place. That was how I thought of it, at least. Somewhere I could think and determine how to go about the few days left of the Baileys' visit to Blackwick. If Mr. Bailey meant to make an offer of marriage, it might well happen soon.

The water reflected the gray of the skies above, and I marveled at how different it could look from day to day. Perhaps that was what drew me to it—it was a source of variation in a life that had come to feel painfully predictable and monotonous.

A wave crashed in front of me, soaking my dress nearly up to my knees, and I picked up the sides as I hurried backwards and out of the water, the heavy fabric adhering to my legs.

I walked back to where my boots lay and took a seat next to them, giving a little shiver at the feel of the cold sand under me. It was a thrill after so many days of being indoors. Sometimes I thought continuous comfort deadened me to feeling. I had been raised in a Scottish baronial home with a great deal of comfort, but it had always been countered by the freedom I was afforded to run wild with our tenants, all of whom lived with a great deal more privation than I. I had waded in frigid streams, milked coos, helped harvest barley and turnips—things that would have made Lady Bailey stare.

The crunch of sand sounded behind me, and I whipped around to see Theo walking toward me. He wore a somber expression, though he attempted a smile as he approached.

"I thought I might find you here," he said, taking a seat beside me.

I felt the familiar rush of nerves he always elicited, and I pushed it away, making room for him, as though the entire beach surrounding us was not desolate.

He sat with his legs bent at the knees, arms wrapped around them while I buried my toes in the sand, keenly aware of my state of relative undress. I wasn't sure why Theo had come or how he had even known to come, but I didn't ask. I simply kept staring forward, watching the rhythmic and relentless rolling of the waves toward the shore, as gray water burst into white froth over and over again.

We sat in silence for a few minutes, and I wondered if he

would perhaps leave before he had said anything beyond his initial words.

"Do you ever wish you could go back?" he asked.

I looked over at him, wondering if he was speaking of Scotland, but he wasn't looking at me. His eyes were forward, taking on a grayish hue as they reflected the water and skies in front of him.

"To childhood." He turned his head to meet my gaze. It was as if he had known the train of my thoughts before his arrival.

"All the time."

His eyes narrowed. "Really?"

I let out a laugh that he should be so suspicious of my answer. "Aye, really." I knew why *I* wished to return to childhood, but did Theo wish for such a thing? He had money, position, freedom. "Ye wish for it too?"

He sucked in a deep breath, his shoulders rising in a shrug along with it. "Everything was more simple then. Everything my heart desired was well within reach, and my decisions affected almost no one but myself. I could play here with you and Di and Valentine and immerse myself in the imaginary for hours at a time."

I looked over at the rock we had played on so often. "But now ye're *livin'* what we could only dream of then. Is that not better than pretendin'?"

His brows contracted. "Sometimes. Sometimes it is the best feeling in the world—standing at the helm of a ship with nothing but water before you and a ship full of men relying on you to take them somewhere safely." His lips turned down at the side. "And then sometimes I am not even certain I *like* sailing anymore."

"That canna be true," I said.

"It is, though. These past few days, I have even considered leaving the Navy."

I looked over at him, thinking of what Valentine said about him losing his love of sailing. "But you love the sea."

"I do. But I do not love the death or the battle that comes with it. Or the feeling that I will never be enough."

"Enough for whom?" I paused. "For yer father?"

There was quiet for a moment, a confirmation in the silence.

It was precisely what I had been feeling all these years—that who I was, where I came from, the things I wanted, were not enough. Even my father, who had loved me dearly, had made me feel that way, for he had sent me to Mrs. Westwood's in the hopes of making me fit for a husband.

Theo readjusted, stretching his legs out in front of him and resting his weight on his palms. He let his head fall back so that he looked up at the sky.

I watched him for a moment, the lashes that rested against his face in a crescent, the line of his jaw and the curve of his neck. Whatever he felt or did not feel for me, he was impossible not to admire. He struck the fine balance of leader and friend—the balance his father seemed incapable of. "Ye *are* enough, Theo."

He looked over at me, his eyes searching mine as the breeze ruffled his hair.

It was the same way he had looked at me since his return that had set my heart pumping and made me think he wished for more than he did. I couldn't afford to pay it any heed. "Do ye ken yer mother worried for ye?"

"What do you mean?"

I drew on the sand at my side with a finger, forming a swirl. "She thought ye were too hard on yerself—that yer father expected too much of ye."

With a sigh, Theo fell silent and pensive.

"She just wanted ye to be happy, Theo. Whatever that means. She seemed preoccupied by that near the end—ensurin' her children were all happy. If the Navy isna leading to that, could ye not find something else to do at sea?"

He gave a light chuckle. "Like what? Join the merchant navy?"

I lifted my shoulders. "Why not?"

He looked at me, his smile fading slightly, as though he had never truly considered anything but rising in the ranks.

I held his gaze. "If it appeals to ye, I see no reason why ye shouldna pursue it."

He shook his head. "My father would be furious. You know how he views that."

I remembered the conversation between the admiral and Lady Bailey well. "Aye, I ken."

"A gentleman should not be on a merchant ship, under the employ of heaven only knows whom."

I nodded. "I suppose ye'll have to decide how much ye let yer father's sentiments guide yer life. He means well. Neither of us doubt that. But are ye livin' his dreams or yer own, Theo? Do ye have any desire to become an admiral? Or Lord of the Fleet?" I felt suddenly nervous. Had I overstepped? Perhaps he would resent how frankly I was speaking.

But he didn't look angry. He merely looked pensive, and I decided to continue.

"I've lived my life tryin' to please others, too, and I'm tired of it. When we live our lives tryin' to avoid disappointin' others, we end up disappointin' ourselves most." I felt my throat catch. Why did it require saying it to Theo for me to realize the truth for myself? "Ye're bound for greatness, Theo. I've known that from the first time I met ye. But it's up to *you* to decide what that greatness looks like."

The side of his mouth turned up in a rueful half-smile. "Where were you when I needed this wisdom a few years ago?"

"Busy doing the same thing as you—tryin' to please everyone else." Him more than anyone.

He gave a sympathetic grimace, and his gaze traveled past me. "Do you remember when we used to play in that cave over there?" He pointed to it, and though I didn't need to turn to see what he meant, I did so. "You told us we could keep away the water wraiths and the kelpies if we made a place for the brownies to live."

I laughed softly and nodded. "Aye, I remember."

"You conveniently failed to mention that kelpies inhabit lochs, not the sea."

"Och, and ye're an expert in Scottish folklore now, are ye?"

He cocked a brow, his eyes glinting playfully at me. "You might be surprised what I learned from my Scottish sailors."

"I reckon I *would* be." I thought of the houses in the cave now—the ones I had dreamed of showing the Baileys, and how Mrs. Bailey had destroyed them. "Come." I pushed myself up from the sand.

He looked up at me, a slight question in his eyes, but he followed suit, brushing off his breeches as I did the same with my dress.

We walked toward the cave together, his boots and my bare feet leaving a strange pair of tracks behind us. We reached the entrance, and I led the way between a few of the larger rocks that protected the cave from the elements.

"Take care not to frighten the brownies," I said, trying to diffuse my nerves as he joined me before the little homes made of sand, sticks, rocks, and shells.

His mouth opened in surprise as he stared at them. He looked to me. "You made these?"

I nodded.

His lips drew into a smile, and he stepped up to one, crouching before it and touching a soft finger to the shells I had used to make the roof. "This is amazing, Elena. And a far cry above the ones we made." He looked up at me, a bit of awe in his eyes.

I shrugged, trying not to mind my immense pleasure in his reaction. I felt . . . weightless. No one had seen these houses until now, and having Theo react to them so positively grew my confidence. It made me wonder why I had taken so much trouble to hide parts of myself. "I've had a great deal more practice since ye left."

He stood up beside me, his arm brushing against mine. "It is like stepping back into our childhood."

Our childhood. It was strange to know he thought of it that way.

He surveyed the houses. "Have you spotted any brownies, then? Should I be thanking them for my safety at sea?"

"I've yet to spot one," I said.

"What a shame," he said. "You deserve *some* reward for this work." He looked to the houses again and then out to the waves. "Do the waves not destroy them?"

"From time to time," I responded. "I reckon they'll be gone in a matter of days when the tide comes up."

"And then what?"

I lifted my shoulders. "I start over, as soon as the tide's gone back out." I thought of all the times I had been obliged to begin again.

"Can I help you next time?" he asked. "I have no skill, of course, but I should like to see how you work."

I hesitated a moment. Doing something like Theo suggested would hardly be proper if I became engaged to Mr. Bailey. Even now, having the two of us here, together and alone, was not in abidance with Mrs. Westwood's dictates.

"Or perhaps it is something you prefer to do alone," he said quickly.

I frowned. "I dinna ken. I've never built them with anyone else. No one even knows of them. Except you now." I glanced at him. "In the beginnin', they were a piece of home—a piece of my childhood, like ye said. And later, they helped me settle my heart and gather my thoughts after spendin' time watchin' your mother in the sickroom. 'Twas hard for me to watch her suffer."

He grimaced. "I can imagine, and I can never repay you for that, Elena. I have been reading through the records you kept, and they are invaluable—something I will always treasure."

"I'm glad for it," I said genuinely. "They *should* be treasured. Yer mother was a remarkable woman, and she deserves to be remembered."

Theo nodded somewhat absently, his eyes fixed on me, as though his thoughts were only partially on his mother. "You know, when I first saw you upon my return, I thought you changed almost beyond recognition. But I was wrong. You are very much the same Elena I always knew. I am glad for it."

I swallowed, my heart pounding. The Elena he had always known was the one who had slipped that humiliating letter into his trunk. How could he say he was glad to find me unchanged when he had left me to hope and hope for a response but never offer one?

A little crab scuttled out from behind one of the rocks inside the cave, sidling over toward the houses. Theo crouched down to watch it more closely, glancing up at me to smile.

I couldn't even manage one. Nor could I manage to withhold the question that had been weighing on my mind all these years. I had to ask. "Why did ye never respond?"

Theo turned toward me, his brows contracting together and his smile wavering. "Respond?"

"To my letter." I took in a deep breath, readying myself for his answer.

He rose to his feet. "What letter?"

A wave of frustration rushed over me at the questioning tone. "The one I sent ye off with the last time ye were home. In yer trunk."

His brows contracted even more, and he looked at me as

though trying to understand whether it was some sort of joke. "I don't know what you mean, Elena. I never had such a letter."

"I put it there meself, Theo. On top of everythin'."

He shook his head slowly. "I have been through that trunk a hundred times, Elena. I know every item in it. There was never any letter."

I stared at him, not sure whether to believe him. Was he trying to pretend ignorance to avoid my anger at how he had treated me? But his expression of bafflement was too genuine.

He put a hand over his heart. "I swear it, Elena."

My heart beat vigorously in my chest as I stared at him. I could hardly comprehend it—all those days of disappointment with no word from him, until I had been obliged to face the fact that nothing ever *would* come. That humiliation had been both creeping and crushing. It had lingered for a long time. It lingered even now.

He lifted his shoulders, brows furrowed deeply. "Perhaps one of the lieutenants stole it as a prank." He shook his head. "No, I would have seen it before then, for my father and I stayed in Dover that first night, and I went through every—" His gaze flew to mine.

I stilled, almost certain we were having the same thought.

"My father," he said. His eyes were searching my face, though his thoughts were clearly elsewhere.

"He slipped a few items from his study into my trunk just before we left for Dover."

I put my hands to my stomach, clenching the fabric tightly. The knowledge that Theo had read my infatuated ramblings had been torture enough, but any concern for that was immediately eclipsed at the realization that it was the admiral who might have read them. I shut my eyes tightly. I might die of shame right there.

"What did it say?" he asked.

Eyes still closed, I shook my head from side to side. The last thing I wanted to do was remember the precise words and what the admiral would have thought of them—thought of *me*.

Theo's hands grasped mine. "What is it, Elena?"

I shook my head again and again.

"It cannot have been so very bad, surely," he said.

I opened my eyes, staring at him. "But it can, Theo. It *was*."

He looked at me uncomprehending, disbelieving, and his hold on my hands tightened.

I gripped them in return, needing him to understand my distress and dismay. "'Twas a pages-long"—I struggled with how to describe it— "*theatrical* declaration of my love for ye."

His hold slackened, his eyes widening. "It . . . it was?"

I nodded, and to my chagrin, emotion began to bubble up inside me. Was it the humiliation of knowing the admiral had read my biggest regret? The fact that this was my first time admitting the letter aloud? The memory of all the pain and grief it had caused me?

Now that the admission had come out, though, I found myself unable to stop the rest. "I begged ye to respond, even if 'twas to tell me there was no hope at all. I *begged*, Theo, like my life depended on it." I didn't know whether I was trying to convince him just how terrible his father reading the letter was or to make him understand what I had been through. Perhaps both.

A spark of hope ignited in my eyes. "Do ye think he's forgotten it? 'Twas seven years ago, after all, and he's had a great deal on his mind. Or perhaps he kens 'twas a childish mistake."

Theo had been staring almost blankly at me this whole time, our hands still clasped between us as we stood just inside the cave, but he flinched at those last words.

"Was it?"

"Was it what?" I swallowed, afraid he was asking the question I feared he was.

"A childish mistake?" he asked softly.

Panic bloomed inside me. I couldn't answer that. "I should never have written ye a secret letter," I said, hoping to evade the implicit meaning in his question.

"And what you expressed *in* that letter," he prodded. "Those feelings. Were they a mistake too? Something long since left behind?"

My heart beat against my chest like stormy waves upon the rocks. When Theo had first returned, I had sworn to myself that, if he ever spoke of the letter, I would laugh at the memory as a relic of yore, that I would never give him the satisfaction of knowing how his rejection had affected me.

But I was tired of pretending. I was tired of carrying the burden of my feelings and the shame of the past alone. My voice caught in my throat, and all I could manage was a faint shake of the head as my eyes filled, blurring my vision.

Theo's hands tightened around mine for a moment. He let go of one, bringing a hand to my cheek and wiping the tear with a thumb.

His hand lingered on my cheek as his eyes looked into mine intently. "I would have written to you, Elena," he whispered. "If I had known, I would have written."

He leaned his head into mine, simultaneously catching my lips and my breath. I should have expected a sailor to taste of the sea, but the hint of salt in the kiss took me by surprise. I lifted my free hand to his jaw, pulling him closer to me, wanting more, as though I could channel the essence of Theo into me through this kiss.

He let go of my other hand, bringing it to my cheek, securing our lips together more surely. The breeze whipped my wet dress against my legs, and I shivered, letting my hand drop from his cheek to grasp his warm shirt as I kissed Theo with seven years' worth of feeling.

He wrapped his arms about me, pulling me into the warmth of his chest, and my shivers immediately fled. I had dreamt of kissing Theo—of him kissing *me*—for years, but my imagination, wild and infatuated as it had once been, had failed to do justice to the experience. The intimacy of being wrapped up in one another's arms with the walls of the cave cradling us on one side and the wide expanse of the sea on the other was something my mind could never have concocted on its own.

A wave crashed on the nearby rocks, and the spray sprinkled our faces, a shock of cold amidst the heat of connection. We pulled apart, and I shivered again.

He smiled at me crookedly, then looked down at my damp dress. "You could not resist going into the water, could you?"

I shook my head, wondering if his heart was beating as quickly as mine or his breath coming as quickly.

"Elena!" a muffled voice called somewhere in the distance.

Chapter Fourteen

Our heads whipped around. Diana stood twenty yards away, hand cupped around her mouth as though this was not the first time she had called.

I glanced at Theo, who looked as surprised as I did, though there was none of the red in his cheeks I felt gathering on my own. I had no doubt at all she had witnessed our kiss—even if she had not, our proximity undoubtedly betrayed us.

Diana walked toward us and we toward her. As the distance between us lessened, her gaze shifted between us, more curious and surprised than condemnatory. What would she say?

"I was sent to find you." She stopped a few feet from us and cocked a brow. "And a good thing, I think, for Mr. Bailey volunteered initially."

I swallowed, feeling the air grow thick as the implications of what had just happened settled over me.

"Admiral Bailey and Arthur have just arrived," she said.

My mouth opened. "My brother Arthur?"

She nodded, and I stared. I hadn't had word from Arthur in more than two months, and now he was *here*?

"We should go," she said. "Admiral Bailey does not look like the sort of man who likes to be kept waiting."

Theo looked at me for a moment, then turned and hurried away from us toward the place I had left my boots in the sand. I glanced at Diana, wondering what she thought of the fact that I had taken them off. Theo brought them back, and I felt a surge of embarrassment at the intimacy of being handed my stockings and boots with an audience.

"Ye dinna have to wait," I said to Theo as I took them in hand. In fact, I hoped they wouldn't. I needed a moment to process everything.

He shook his head, and I turned away from him, setting my boots on the ground and attempting to pull on my stocking while standing. I wobbled from side to side, and someone grasped my upper arm to help stabilize me—Theo.

I shot him a quick, civil smile, ever-conscious of Diana nearby, and pulled on the other sock before shoving my feet into my boots, not even bothering to lace them before I let down my skirts.

The three of us made our way up the path in silence, and I was left to wonder whether Theo was contemplating what had just passed between us or what the arrival of Admiral Bailey meant, particularly given the conversation we had shared on the beach.

The sand that stuck between my toes and along my ankles rubbed my skin as we made the walk, but not for the world would I have stopped. Diana said nothing, but I knew her well enough to anticipate she would have plenty to say when the opportunity to do so privately arose.

The silence was painful and even a bit ominous, though, and I could barely stand it any longer by the time we reached the manicured lawn behind the hall.

"Admiral Bailey and Arthur arrived together?" I asked.

"Yes. Apparently they met at some club or another while in

London and discovered they had the same destination. Your brother had intended to come by post chaise, but the admiral offered him a place in his carriage."

Of all the times Arthur could arrive, today was certainly the least propitious.

Theo and I had kissed, but we had not had a chance to discuss what exactly that kiss meant. And now I would be obliged to interact with Mr. Bailey again. I felt a bit sick at the thought.

A servant opened the door to Blackwick Hall, and Theo waited for Diana and me to pass through first.

Admiral Donovan was waiting in the entry hall, and my muscles tensed at the sight of him, the realization Theo and I had come to together—that he had read my letter—rushing in on me again.

"Admiral Bailey is taking some refreshment in the parlor," Admiral Donovan said to Theo. "He wishes for you to join him. You too, Diana." He turned toward me. "If I may have a word with you, Elena. Your brother had an urgent letter to write and should be down in a few minutes."

I gave a nod, though my muscles were rigid.

Theo looked at me, hesitating a moment, as though he was reluctant to leave me with his father. I tried to give him my best reassuring but unsuspicious smile, though I was far from feeling reassured myself.

He and Diana made their way to the parlor, while I lingered in the entry hall, waiting for whatever Admiral Donovan needed to say to me in private. He watched his children until they disappeared into the parlor door, then turned to me, wearing his customarily sober expression.

"I apologize, sir, if my brother's arrival has inconvenienced you at all," I said, reverting to the speech he expected from me now. "I had no idea he meant to come here. I had assumed he would go back to Scotland as soon as he was able."

The admiral shook his head. "It is no trouble at all. It is fortunate he was able to make the journey with Admiral Bailey." His gaze became more fixed on me. "The admiral is anxious to meet you."

I forced myself not to squirm or fidget. "Is he?" I hoped it didn't sound as evasive as it felt.

He gave a nod. "It is a match your father would be pleased with."

My conscience writhed. I was sure he was right. My father would be thrilled to know that I was being considered by someone like Mr. Bailey. But I had just kissed Theo.

"The admiral's visit is crucial for Captain Donovan, as you know," he continued. "He cannot afford any . . . distractions." He looked at me meaningfully.

A distraction. That was how Admiral Donovan thought of me. Now and in the past, it seemed.

"Did you take the letter?" I asked, surprised by my own bravery. But just now I was feeling particularly frustrated with my godfather and how he had affected the course of my life. I might have been corresponding with Theo all these years, but instead he had crushed my heart and deprived both Theo and me of . . . of I hardly knew what. It was impossible to fathom how life would have been different if that letter had not disappeared.

His brows knit, but I saw a glint of recognition in his eyes, all the same. "What letter?"

"The letter I put in Theo's trunk when he became a lieutenant."

There was silence as the admiral gave me a measuring look. "Yes."

I was speechless. What could I possibly respond to such an admission?

"The heights Theo can reach are limitless, Elena. But his focus can be quickly deterred by the overabundance of sentiment he inherited from his mother—I saw it from early on with her illness. He would often neglect his duties in favor of the sickroom."

My hands clenched at my sides as I stared at the admiral. "That is to his credit, surely."

His lips pinched together, betraying that he did not agree. "There is no credit to be had in neglecting one's duties. He would not be where he is today if I had not taken decisive action and sent my wife to Blackwick."

I looked at him in bafflement. Was he saying that he had forced his ailing wife home because he feared how it would affect his son's naval career? Evidently, Valentine's assertions had *not* been based in cynicism.

"It was for her own good, too, of course," he said, as if reading my thoughts. He cleared his throat. "The point is, I hope you will not urge him to do anything that might be detrimental to his career or that would counter the hard work he has put into distinguishing himself."

The humiliation of this conversation and the anger at hearing the admiral speak so flippantly about his wife's protracted illness made the blood run hot in my veins. I felt for Mrs. Donovan, being married to a man who could see nothing beyond the way others affected his naval prospects.

"Your son will distinguish himself *because of*, not in spite of his heart, sir. But you may rest easy. Now that I know how you view my presence here, I will relieve you of it as soon as may be arranged."

"Elena," the admiral said in his deep voice, a hint of supplication softening it. "I am your godfather. I promised your father I would do everything in my power to arrange your future. Mr. Bailey will care for you in a way that is simply not possible for someone in the Navy. You must trust me on this, for I speak from experience. I will be discussing things with your brother as soon as both of us have a free moment. Now that he is home, he should be involved in any marriage talks, of course."

"Nay, sir," I hurried to say. I didn't want him to speak with Arthur about such things, especially not after what had just happened.

The admiral looked at me with tight lips and a mixture of frustration and disappointment in his eyes.

My emotions, first stirred up with Theo, then with Diana's sudden appearance, filled my body like a rising tide, thickening my throat, making my cheeks burn, and bringing tears to my eyes.

"There ye are!"

I whipped my head around toward the stairs and found myself watching Arthur descend them with his broad smile, looking far older than the last time I had seen him—fuller in the jaw and shoulders, brown hair cropped short, whiskers extending down the side of his face.

"Arthur!" I said, hurrying toward him and wrapping my arms around him. The embrace only heightened my overwrought emotions. It had been so long since I had been with family.

"I will leave the two of you." The admiral gave a nod and made his way toward the parlor.

I stepped back and brushed away at the tears that had escaped, hoping Arthur would assume they were owing to his arrival. "What're ye doin' here?"

He put out his hands, palms up. "I've come ta take ye home, of course." He spoke with a brogue that made mine sound soft in comparison, and hearing it made my heart ache.

"Home," I repeated. My conversation with Admiral Donovan made me want to insist we be on our way as soon as possible. But I couldn't. At least not just yet. "Ye've come at a strange time, Arthur."

His brows went up, and I pulled my lips in. I didn't know how much to tell him.

"I'm in a bit of a situation here."

He cocked a brow, waiting for me to expound.

I said nothing, and he narrowed his eyes as though he might discover what I meant by looking at me intently enough. I couldn't bring myself to tell him, not with the muddle everything was in. I didn't even know what would happen next.

"What sort of situation?" he asked. "I only came intendin' ta stay two or three days, Lena. I need ta get back ta Benleith."

I nodded quickly. "I willna need more than that." I had no idea whether I would be leaving with Arthur back to Scotland or remaining here, but I only had a bit of time to make such a decision. I needed to sort things out myself first.

"Och, it does my heart good ta see ye," I said. "More handsome than ever ye are."

He grinned and turned in a full circle so I could see him. "I canna say the same for *you*." He kicked a foot at the bottom of my dress, still dark with the damp of the sea. When it dried, it would be lighter than the rest of the fabric, saturated with seawater. The thought of salt brought my kiss with Theo to mind, stirring heat in my bones.

"Is that what ye learned at that fine finishin' school of yers?" Arthur asked, tweaking my braid.

I bit the inside of my lip, tucking a lock of hair behind my ear, where it resisted my efforts, popping back out.

"I'm only teasin', Lena," Arthur said. "I'd have been disappointed if I'd come here ta find ye a proper lass. But yer accent isna what it used ta be."

"Arthur," I said quickly, suddenly remembering what problems his arrival would cause for me. "About that. I need ta tell ye—"

The door to the parlor opened down the corridor, and people began emerging—Mr. Bailey and Diana first, followed by Theo and the man I assumed could only be Admiral Bailey, with Admiral Donovan and Lady Bailey at the rear.

My eyes widened, and for a moment, I considered running to

the stairs, disappearing before any of the Baileys could see the state of me.

"Miss MacKinnon," Mr. Bailey said with a smile that made my conscience wince. His eyes flicked to my hair, and I resisted the impulse to flatten it. It would be a useless endeavor. "We feared you might have gone upstairs already. I am glad to be wrong. I wished to introduce you to my father, Admiral Henry Bailey."

The admiral stepped forward from his place beside Theo, who had his hands clasped behind his back. He wore a somber expression.

"Good day to you, Miss MacKinnon."

I made my curtsy just as Mr. Bailey spoke again. "And Mother, I do not think you met Miss MacKinnon's brother yet, Arthur MacKinnon, Baron of Benleith."

Arthur made a fine bow, and Lady Bailey inclined her head in acknowledgement of the gesture.

"A Scottish baron, is it?" Lady Bailey said.

"Aye, my lady," Arthur responded.

She smiled, but the curl of her lip showed just what she thought of his brogue and his inferior barony, for Scottish baronies could be bought and sold, unlike English ones, which were inherited. Neither did they offer their holders the title of *lord*. Had she thought me the sister of a peer this entire time?

"I'm pleased ta meet ye, Lady Bailey," Arthur said. "Yer husband is a good man, and I'm grateful ta him for lettin' me join him in his carriage."

Lady Bailey was blinking as though being assaulted, and Arthur's wide smile faltered slightly at the reaction.

"My, what an accent you have," she said with a strained smile. "I had assumed it would be similar to your sister's."

I tensed and couldn't help glancing at Theo and Diana. Diana looked as though she was trying valiantly to control a smile.

Arthur laughed. "My sister once had the strongest brogue in the family."

I forced a laugh, surrendering to the fact that Arthur was determined to destroy whatever pride I had left. "Och," I said in my brogue, "it comes and goes—'tis strongest when I'm with mischief-makers like this one." I gripped my brother's arm more tightly than necessary, and he shot me a look, half-laughing, half-questioning.

Mr. Bailey looked somewhat befuddled, but he was not the type to say as much. Just where he had gained his open personality was even more of a mystery to me now that I had met his father. Admiral Bailey was less severe than Admiral Donovan, and he had done a kindness in bringing my brother here, but he did not seem the type of man to ever be at the center of a lively conversation. As for Lady Bailey, she was looking at me fixedly, her expression far from admiring.

Mr. Bailey filled the somewhat awkward silence. "We were just discussing something in the parlor and wished to come see what the two of you thought of the idea."

I raised my brows, aware of Lady Bailey's eyes on the bottom of my dress. In truth, it seemed as though *everyone's* eyes were on me. "Oh?"

He gestured to Admiral Bailey. "My father mentioned making a trip into Dover to show Captain Donovan the ship he may be taking command of, and I thought it might be an enjoyable thing for all of us to do together—go into Dover, I mean."

I glanced at Theo, who met my eyes, but I couldn't make anything of his expression.

"A fine idea," Arthur said jovially.

"Yes, I would enjoy that," I said.

Mr. Bailey smiled. "It is settled, then. We go to Dover tomorrow."

Chapter Fifteen

The gray skies of earlier that day gave way to angry clouds and an evening rainstorm. After the disheveled way I had presented myself earlier in the day, I was determined to go down to dinner looking precise as a pin—or thirty pins, rather, given the number Hitchen had been obliged to use in my hair to achieve the style she wished for.

A nervous and restless energy coursed throughout my body as we gathered before the meal. Mr. Bailey hovered around me in a somewhat possessive way, while my eyes looked for Theo, who did not arrive until just before we moved to the dining room. His expression was somber, a faint crease between his brows.

His gaze found me, though, as Mr. Bailey offered me his arm, and it lingered for a moment before he shot me a smile that only confirmed to me that he was troubled.

My stomach swam. Did he regret our kiss at the cove? Had his father spoken to him, as well, warning him against me?

I took in a deep breath, trying to put the unwelcome speculation from my mind. I had other pressing matters to see to—deciding what accent to adopt, for example. With Arthur here, my brogue clawed to be free from the Westwoodian grip under which I had maintained it for a week and a half now. He had provided just the impetus—inelegant as it had been—that I needed to make the shift.

So, I liberated my brogue.

Aside from a few initial surprised glances at me, Mr. Bailey seemed not to mind. Lady Bailey, however, wore a pinched look during dinner anytime Arthur or I spoke. I wondered if she truly had trouble understanding either of us or if she simply disliked the sound of Scotland.

Diana sought me out in the drawing room, but we were prevented from any meaningful conversation by the fact that there was no one to engage Lady Bailey if we went off to a corner to speak. I was grateful for that, though, as I had no idea what I should say to Diana when she asked the inevitable questions. I was as confused as she.

When the men joined us a short time later, everyone seemed to congregate around the fire. The slapping of rain on the windowpanes and the muffled rumbling of thunder outside made it feel colder than it truly was.

Admiral Bailey and Theo conversed in low tones in two wingback chairs to the side of the fireplace, while Arthur and Valentine pulled a small table nearby to begin a game of cards. The two of them were an interesting combination, for Arthur was gregarious while Valentine was dour and uncommunicative in the presence of his father.

"What a dreary evening," said Lady Bailey with a glance at the windows.

"Och," said Arthur, "snug and cozy, I call it. There's naught like bein' indoors and around a hot fire when 'tis stormin' out." He smiled broadly. "'Twas nights like tonight when I'd regale the other soldiers with a few stories around the fire ta distract them from the cold."

"What sort of stories?" Diana asked, her head cocking to the side.

Arthur smiled mischievously as he set down a card. "Naught but a wee tale or two about the moss-covered *ghillie dhu* or the caprice of the brownies. Or"—he cocked a brow at her—"if I was feelin' particularly irked that night, I'd tell them about the evils of the Slaugh."

I would never have spoken of such legends in the company of Lady Bailey, but Arthur was not one to worry himself over the opinion of others. I envied him that, even if I couldn't help shifting in my seat and looking around for the reactions of the company.

"The Slaugh?" Diana asked.

"The evil host of fairies that haunts Scotland—our unforgiven dead." Arthur was taking positive delight in conveying such an answer. Far from being frightened, Diana clapped her hands together.

"It is settled, then. You must tell us these stories. It has been years since I heard any Scottish legends."

My muscles tightened.

"Ye ken some already, then?" Arthur asked, impressed.

Diana looked at me, and though I widened my eyes in warning, she ignored it entirely. "Elena terrified all of us that a water wraith should emerge from the sea at any moment. I believe Theo nearly abandoned his idea of continuing in the Navy after that."

Theo's head turned from his conversation with Admiral Bailey at the mention of his name. He looked at Diana questioningly.

"I was just saying how frightened you were of the sea after Elena told us about water wraiths. You wouldn't go to the cove for some time, and I believe you considered giving up the Navy altogether."

Admiral Donovan let out a sound of annoyance, and I

cringed inwardly at the implication that I had done the very thing he feared: nearly distracted Theo from his career.

"I have no patience for superstition," Admiral Donovan said testily.

"I should think not!" Lady Bailey wrapped her shawl more tightly around her shoulders, looking highly offended.

"Like it or not," Theo said, "superstition is alive and well amongst many sailors, and Elena's stories helped me on more than one occasion to better understand the men under my command."

I looked at Theo, wondering that he should choose to defend me at such a moment.

Lady Bailey regarded me with the same pinched lips that she had worn every time her gaze landed upon me that evening. "Surely *you* do not believe such"—she sputtered for a moment—"demonic madness, Miss MacKinnon."

All eyes turned to me. I could have denied it flatly, of course. But the look of sheer repulsion she was directing at me nettled me.

"I canna pretend to understand even the wee bit of the world I have seen," I said, "but I've found value in the myths and legends of my forefathers, regardless of whether they are strictly accurate. All of us seek to explain what we see and experience in the world—doin' so helps us feel a bit more in control, I think—but we tend to look down upon those whose explanations differ from ours."

My eyes found Theo's, which were looking at me intently. His expression took me back to the cove—it seemed ages ago, though it was only a matter of hours—and the feel of his fingers grasping my waist. I pulled my gaze away quickly. I had felt certain of his feelings in that moment, but now, I was far from sure about anything.

"Be that as it may," Admiral Bailey said from beside Theo, "I must agree that superstition has no place on a ship in His

Majesty's Royal Navy—even less place than women, I would dare say. Both are a distraction and lead to mistakes we can ill afford."

Admiral Donovan gave a gruff grunt of assent, and Lady Bailey nodded vigorously.

"I certainly learned *my* lesson," Admiral Donovan said. "My wife's time aboard the *Dominance* was injurious to not only herself but to the focus and morale of the men."

"Surely not," Diana said somewhat hotly. "I believe you are misremembering, Father."

But as her accusation was followed by Lady Bailey recounting various stories of the horrors her acquaintances—and her acquaintances' acquaintances—had experienced on board, the subject of Mrs. Donovan was dropped.

Theo looked more and more stricken as he listened to Lady Bailey, and I wished for just five minutes with him to understand what in heaven's name was in his mind and heart—and what he expected me to do now.

Chapter Sixteen

I woke the next morning with the same unease in my stomach that had been plaguing me for some time now—except for those few minutes at the cove with Theo. But those minutes were beginning to feel like a dream. I almost wondered if I had imagined it all until I inevitably remembered the moments following. Lady Bailey's stares, her dismay at my brogue, and the state of my clothing had been too potent to attribute to a dream.

I had no idea what Theo was feeling—only that he had spent the evening in discussion with Admiral Bailey and looked at me with an expression that made me feel sick. But I had spent too many years wondering what Theo was thinking and feeling. I didn't want to spend any more time wondering.

It was earlier than I usually rose, but I threw off my bedcovers and pulled the bell for Hitchen. I had two days at most before Arthur intended to return to Scotland—with or without me. I needed to use them wisely.

Hitchen helped me into my plain gray muslin, and I begged her to arrange my hair in something quick and simple, reassuring her that I would allow her to change it later. She had become more invested in my coiffures since being instructed by Tait. But Theo was an early riser, and if I wanted any chance of finding him before others rose, it was quickly disappearing.

I found him in the breakfast room, sitting beside Phineas, who had the usual book sitting next to his plate. They had been talking but fell silent and looked to the door, where I hesitated, unsure what to do.

Phineas's eyes flicked from me to Theo and back again. He cleared his throat and took his book in hand. "If you will excuse me, I have some reading to do." He gave a nod to me as he passed by me to leave the room. Phineas was far from being the most social of the Donovan children, but I appreciated his unexpected astuteness.

The door closed behind me, and the air in the room grew suddenly thick.

Theo rose from his chair. "I am glad you came." His eyes held that same look I had noted since Diana came upon us at the cove—guarded and sober. I didn't know what it meant, but I intended to find out. No longer would I guess and wonder.

"I had hoped to find ye here," I said. "I wished to speak with ye."

"And I you." He took a step closer to me, and I felt the pull he exerted on me—the memory of the warmth of his chest, the feel of his lips on mine, the moment when he had reassured me that he would have written to me.

I took a step back, afraid to surrender to what I wanted when all was so evidently not right or settled between us.

"What do ye want, Theo?" I asked abruptly.

His eyebrows contracted slightly, but he took in a deep breath, not responding immediately. The hesitation was more painful than anything he might have said.

I knew what I wanted—I wanted Theo. And I would have told him if he had asked me. I had done as much yesterday, had I not?

"I want to apologize," he finally said.

"Apologize for what?"

He lifted his shoulders. "For being careless, I suppose."

I held his gaze, forcing myself to stay quiet so that he would fill the silence.

"I understand that Bailey intends to make an offer of marriage soon—perhaps today, even."

I had anticipated that it would be soon, but that it might be today was new information. New and unwelcome. I didn't want to marry Mr. Bailey.

"It was wrong of me to kiss you, Elena," he said, brow furrowed. "I did not even pause to consider what it would mean for you—for Bailey."

I swallowed, refusing to let my emotion dominate me, even if Theo *was* apologizing for the time that I hadn't ceased thinking of for more than five minutes since yesterday. "Ye'd still encourage me to marry him, then?" I kept my chin high.

Theo shut his eyes. "Elena, I . . ." His jaw tightened, and he opened his eyes again. "You know what has haunted me? What kept me awake last night?"

I said nothing but held his gaze, refusing to blink, for I knew that the tears would come if I did.

"It was the thought of watching you suffer as my mother did—of being the cause of it, of knowing I might have prevented it but chose instead to be selfish and keep you with me." His lips turned down at the sides, and he wiped a hand over his face, shaking his head from side to side. "I cannot bear it, Elena. I care for you too much. And yesterday, I allowed my feelings for you to overcome what I know to be right."

My hold on my emotions was becoming more tenuous by the second—with every admission that he cared for me. Cared for me but would not *be* with me. My throat was too thick for me to speak.

"Say something," he pleaded.

"What exactly do ye wish for me to say, Theo? My own wishes, my own feelin's have no bearin' on the matter."

"Of course they do."

I shook my head and turned to the chair nearest me, gripping the back of it with my hands.

"Elena." He stepped up behind me, putting a hand on my shoulder. "They *do* matter. It is for your feelings that I am concerned. You heard last night—the rigors and privations of life aboard are no small thing."

I turned to face him, and his hand fell from my shoulder. "And ye think I'd rather be without ye than suffer such discomforts?"

He pursed his lips. "You do not know what you would be agreeing to. You said it yourself—you have never been aboard a ship."

I crossed my arms. "Tell me honestly, Theo. How much of this is about yer father and Admiral Bailey's opinions on the matter of women on board? Are ye afraid to disappoint them?"

Behind his cravat, his throat bobbed. "The Admiralty means to offer me the captaincy on *Kestrel*."

"And you mean to accept," I replied. It wasn't a question.

He lifted his shoulders. "How can I not? To receive a commission at a time like this, when so many men are surviving on meager half-pay? It is an honor. It would ruin my career to say no."

"So, ye see a wife as an impediment to yer career."

"No, Elena." He threw up his hands and took to pacing.

I watched him, saying nothing, contemplating whether I should simply leave. Theo might care for me, but when he gave reason after reason why we could not be together, all I heard were the excuses of a man trying to avoid something he didn't truly want.

Somewhere inside, I was aware of how this interaction would hurt me later. But for now, I was simply tired of being in a constant state of suspension, waiting, wanting, hoping, but never knowing.

Finally, he turned to me, running a hand through his blond hair. "I do not know how to please everyone, Elena."

"That's because ye canna, Theo. *Ye canna* please everyone. Dinna try to please yer father. Dinna try to please Lady Bailey or Admiral Bailey. And for heaven's sake, dinna try to please me. Do what ye feel is right for ye, or ye'll begin a pattern that ye may not be able to stop. Ye may find yourself in twenty years with a son of yer own makin' himself miserable trying to please ye."

I turned and walked to the door, surprised to find that, though my hands shook slightly, the desire to cry had fled. One hand on the doorknob, I stopped. "I spent a great deal of time with yer mother, Theo, and she never spoke with anythin' but fondness of her time on board. She only ever lamented bein' left to ail at home without her husband or sons—unable to be with the ones she loved."

Without looking back, I pulled the door open and left.

Chapter Seventeen

I went directly to Arthur's bedchamber, rapping on the door with a glance down the corridor, my heart still skipping and tumbling from the encounter with Theo.

I had to knock a second time, and just as I began to wonder whether Arthur and I had somehow missed one another between here and the breakfast room, the door opened.

Arthur appeared with a room still shuttered in darkness, rubbing his eyes, shirt unbuttoned and a dressing gown hastily thrown on. "Elena?" he said blinkingly.

"I want to go home," I said.

"What?"

"I want to go home," I repeated.

He rubbed the inside of his eyes. "Och, Lena. Could this not have waited?"

"It's nine o'clock, Arthur. Ye shouldna be asleep at this hour. When can we leave?"

His brows pulled together in annoyance. "We leave the day after tomorrow. 'Tis when our ship leaves port."

"We're sailin'?" I asked, forgetting my problems for a moment.

"Aye. 'Twill cost less than goin' by carriage."

I sucked in a breath. I would finally go on a ship. But the day after tomorrow . . . that was an unbearable lifetime away.

"There's not another one we could take?"

"Nay," he said baldly, some of the sleepiness fleeing his eyes as he directed an evaluative look at me. "Besides, I told Bailey I'd come to Dover today."

I sighed. Arthur was one of the best-humored people I knew, but he could be terribly stubborn about peculiar things.

"Why are ye so anxious to leave all of a sudden?" he asked.

I gave a scoffing laugh. I was not about to tell Arthur the extent of what had just happened in the breakfast parlor. "I've been at Blackwick Hall for *years*, Arthur. I'm anxious to be home."

He narrowed his eyes slightly. He meant to pry further. I could see that, and I had no idea how much he had gathered about my situation at Blackwick since his arrival.

"The day after tomorrow, then," I said in an attempt to ward off any of his questions. At any rate, I still needed to speak with Mr. Bailey to explain things to him. I knew now that I could not marry him, rational as the choice might be. I needed time at home—time to decide what I wanted my future to be and *who* I wanted to be. I had tried and failed to be the proper lady Mrs. Westwood had taught me to become, and I did not wish to live my life being looked down upon by Lady Bailey or her husband. But Mr. Bailey was an innocent casualty of my foolishness, and I did not relish the thought of telling him that. It had to be done, though.

True to my word, I returned to my bedchamber to allow Hitchen to arrange my hair for the expedition to Dover, hoping that, sometime during the course of the day, I might be able to speak to Mr. Bailey.

The men decided to ride, providing needed exercise for the horses in the stables, while the women settled on traveling in the Donovans' chaise. The men stood talking together by the horses while we awaited Lady Bailey's arrival. I didn't know whether to grudge her her tardiness or wish that I had stayed at my toilette longer, for it was all I could do to avoid Theo's gaze.

"Why don't we wait in the chaise, Elena?" Diana smiled at the men and pulled me by the hand toward the equipage, where the postilion hurried to open the door. I knew what Diana was doing and why, but as the discussion ahead was inevitable and I found being in Theo's company taxed my heart, I did not resist.

As soon as the door was shut, she sat on the edge of her seat to narrow the distance between us, looking at me with a hitched brow. "Well?" She kept her voice lower than usual, and the muffled conversation I could hear outside the chaise reassured me that we would not be heard.

"Well what?" It was useless, I knew that. But I hardly knew what to say to Diana. This was something I had kept from her for years.

She shot me an unamused look, her head tilted to the side. "You mean to pretend nothing happened yesterday?"

"If ye'll let me, aye."

She shook her head. "What I saw was not *nothing*."

My mind was inevitably taken back to the kiss, and I wondered if I would ever be able to forget how it felt to be with Theo like that—to taste what I had wanted and dreamed of for so long.

"'Twas nothin' because nothin' will come of it," I said, holding her gaze.

"What, precisely, is *it*?"

I remained silent, for there was no good answer to her question. Or at least no simple one.

Her lips pinched together in discontent with my lack of communicativeness. "I know you, Elena. You are not the sort of person to kiss or trifle with men. Is the connection between you and Theo recent? Or have I been more blind than I thought possible?"

I chewed the inside of my lip for a moment, debating how much to tell her. Part of me wanted to continue resisting her efforts to have the information from me, but the rest of me was tired of keeping a secret that was affecting me so deeply. Besides, there simply *was* no pretending after what Diana had seen. It would be better to confess it all, or she was likely to go to Theo with her questions, and I would rather she didn't.

As quickly and emotionlessly as possible, I explained things to her, glancing at the door of the chaise every time there was a lull in the conversation outside.

When I reached the point in the story of her coming upon us at the cove, I stopped, thrown off by the smile on her face.

"I must be the greatest dunce in all of history not to have guessed any of this—though, I should not have *had* to, for you should have told me everything from the beginning—something I shall never forgive you for, except that you are to be my sister now, and one must always forgive family—"

"Diana," I said loudly, swallowing away the lump in my throat at the picture her words painted.

She stopped talking.

I took a breath. "He doesna want me."

Her brows snapped together. "Nonsense. That is not what I saw."

"'Twas a mistake. He wants me to marry Mr. Bailey."

She waved a dismissive hand. "More nonsense. A man like Theo does not kiss a woman when he wants her to marry someone else."

I glanced at the window shade, afraid Theo might hear. "He's bein' offered the captaincy, and he refuses to take a woman on board. He doesna want to repeat what happened to yer mother."

"What happened to my—" She snapped her mouth shut. "Ill

or not, my mother was at her happiest aboard a ship. She didn't truly begin to decline until she came home, but of course neither my father nor my brothers understand that, for they were not here to see it." She took in a breath. "I will speak to Theo."

I grabbed her arm frantically. "No, Di!"

Surprise flashed on her face, and I loosened my hold on her arm. "Please dinna interfere."

Her gaze searched mine, uncomprehending.

"A man shouldna have to be convinced to marry a woman," I said simply. I felt the emotion rise in my throat at my pathetic words—my pathetic situation.

"But, Elena—"

The door opened, and Lady Bailey appeared, taking her husband's arm as he handed her up into the chaise.

Our conversation was necessarily halted, and Diana shot a tight-lipped, resigned look at me as Lady Bailey took a seat next to her. A waft of potent lavender perfume filled the chaise, and I blinked, pulling back farther into the squabs. I was not fond of lavender.

It had been some time since I had gone any farther than the village nearest Blackwick Hall. In attempt to keep my mind off Theo, I looked through the window at the passing countryside, allowing Diana and Lady Bailey to assume the burden of conversing. Tomorrow I would see places much more unfamiliar to me as Arthur and I began our journey home. I felt a mixture of anticipation and nerves at the thought. What sort of future awaited me in Scotland? Would it feel familiar or foreign? Here I had been too Scottish; would I be too English there after so many years away?

The port at Dover was a bustling hub of activity, with smaller vessels in port and larger ones anchored farther off in the distance. We took the chaise and horses to the inn closest to the dockyard, and I found Mr. Bailey waiting to offer me his arm when I stepped down from the equipage, bonnet secured on my head again.

It was a fine day, a smattering of white clouds making the blue sky behind them look all the more vibrant. The sun created a bright sheen on the water, giving the impression of a mirror in some places.

Theo and Admiral Bailey walked up toward the chaise, and I felt the former's eyes on me. I was not trying to be unkind or vengeful by avoiding Theo, though it was probable it seemed that way to him. I was merely protecting myself.

Lady Bailey took her husband's arm and stepped down from the carriage. I watched as she passed Theo, who blinked and reared back slightly—at the perfume, I assumed.

Lady Bailey looked around and pulled a face, making a faint noise of disgust.

Mr. Bailey smiled sympathetically. "Mother was never fond of ports."

"Malodorous places," she said, bringing her wrist to her nose and inhaling. "I wore my strongest perfume in preparation."

I was well aware of that.

We made our way from The George Inn along the paved path that led to the dockyard, Admiral Bailey and Theo leading the way while the rest of us configured ourselves in twos behind, Mr. Bailey and I paired together.

I let my eyes run over the assortment of boats and ships that sat still amongst a city of seemingly ceaseless movement. The masts towered above us like sentinels, and I took in the scent of the salty sea and fish with interest—and no perfume.

"You look entranced, Miss MacKinnon," Mr. Bailey said.

I pulled my eyes away and smiled somewhat sheepishly. "A bit, aye. I've always wanted to sail somewhere."

"Really?" He looked puzzled by my comment.

"I grew up hearin' stories of sailin' from my father—and the Donovan men, as well."

"Much like I did," he commented. "But any desire *I* had to sail was cured the first time I had the opportunity to fulfill it. Perhaps it will be the same for you."

I tried for a smile, wondering if he was correct. Was all my hankering after life at sea misplaced? Perhaps I *was* a creature of comforts like Mr. Bailey. But as I looked out over the array of ships and boats, I didn't think so. Like these motionless ships in port, I had been stagnant and without a sail for so long.

"Which of these vessels appeals to you most?" he asked.

I tried to picture myself on the decks of the ones we were passing, pretending I had the choice of which one to board. My eyes alighted on one in particular. It was one of the largest in port, though not nearly the size of the two anchored farther out. It must have been stunning when it first took to the seas, painted in golds and blues as it was, though the colors had faded and much of the paint was chipping away. Its three masts towered above, shorn of their sails in a complex bouquet of rigging, but I could envision how it would look with the sails billowing in the wind.

I pointed to it. "That one."

Admiral Bailey and Theo stopped just ahead of us, conferring together as they looked out toward the ships anchored in the distance.

Mr. Bailey and I came to a stop behind them, and he looked to the ship I indicated, his brows raising. "Hm. An unexpected choice."

I tilted my head, inspecting it another time and imagining all the stories it might tell. "It looks as though it has served well—and earned the rest it is now having."

He smiled and gave a nod. "Indeed, it does."

His smile stirred up guilt in my stomach. I needed to tell him.

I glanced over at Theo, whom I found watching us, a hint of

pain in his eyes. I looked away before my own pain betrayed *me*. He had chosen this.

The admiral pulled a pocket watch from inside his blue coat and looked at it. "They should be here any minute." Squinting his wrinkled eyes, he looked out again toward the ships. "Ah, yes. I see the boat. Just there."

But Theo was not watching. His own eyes were narrowed, looking somewhere behind me. They lit up suddenly, and a smile stretched across his face.

"Excuse me a moment, Admiral." With a distracted nod, gaze still fixed on the same spot, he made his way past Mr. Bailey, me, and the others.

I turned to watch, too curious not to. Theo ran over to a man coming down the gangway of the ship I had pointed to. The man was attired in rough and worn clothing and carried a crate on his shoulder. At the sight of Theo, though, he hurried to set it down, and the two of them embraced. The happiness on Theo's face—the way it made his eyes wrinkle at the sides and pulled his mouth out into a smile of unfettered joy—did something to my heart.

I looked to Diana and her father, both of whom were watching with as much surprise as I had been.

"A happy reunion," Mr. Bailey commented.

I glanced at him and realized he was watching me rather than Theo. "It certainly appears so."

Theo and the stranger remained talking for a few long minutes until the boat that Admiral Bailey had mentioned arrived and Admiral Donovan was obliged to alert Theo to the fact.

The two men exchanged a few more words and a handshake after which Theo returned, apologizing to Admiral Bailey for keeping him waiting.

"Povey and I served together as lieutenants a few years ago," he explained, somewhat breathless.

"And he works on a merchant ship now?" Admiral Bailey's disapproval was apparent in both his tone and expression.

Theo nodded and looked to the man who had rowed the boat to the docks. "Shall we be on our way?"

Admiral Bailey gave a grunt, and Theo nimbly lowered himself into the boat, offering a hand to the admiral. Once he, too, was settled, they turned their attention back to the docks.

Theo's eyes moved to me, a wary, questioning look in them. "Would you like to come?" His voice was tentative.

"A capital idea," Mr. Bailey said approvingly. "She was just telling me how she has long wished to be on a ship but has never had the opportunity."

I shifted a bit—between knowing I would have the opportunity of sailing tomorrow, the prospect of seeing a real warship myself, and the thought of being in a boat with Theo for the journey to *and* from that ship, I hardly knew what to say.

"Come along, then, both of you," said Admiral Bailey, motioning to his son and me.

Not feeling prepared to counter the admiral's command, I allowed Mr. Bailey to escort me to the edge of the dock, where Theo waited, hand extended toward me.

My heart somersaulted, but there was no refusing with the audience we had. I tried to pretend nonchalance as I stepped onto the planks and he set a steadying hand to my waist as the boat listed from side to side. When he took his hand away, its presence lingered, just as it had after our kiss.

I thanked him quietly, avoiding his eye, then found a seat as Mr. Bailey climbed down. I remembered Theo saying how strange it was to have solid ground beneath his feet after so much time at sea, and I smiled slightly at the novel sensation of imbalance.

Once Mr. Bailey had taken his seat beside me, Theo pushed us away from the docks, and those we were leaving behind waved to us. Diana and I caught eyes, hers expressive with a keen understanding of the situation I found myself in.

The men took up the oars, and we began on our way toward the *Kestrel*. Water lapped up against the sides of the boat, sending a few drops onto my face or dress every now and then, and I watched in secret delight as the distance between us and the docks grew.

Soon, nothing but water surrounded us, glinting and sparkling in the sunlight, as the men's arms worked in tandem. I tried as well as I could to avoid looking past Mr. Bailey at Theo's broad shoulders or the way the vein in his neck pulsed at the exertion of fighting the current. Instead I focused my gaze on the sea, the oars dipping in and reemerging a moment later, dripping with water.

Mr. Bailey's breath was coming quickly, his brows furrowed in focus and face turning red from the toil of rowing.

"May I?" I asked.

He turned his head to look at me, and realizing what I was asking, hesitated for a moment. "There is no need for you to row, Miss MacKinnon."

"But I want to," I replied.

He gave a little smile and pulled the oars out of the water, setting them in their holders, and ceding his place to me.

Theo looked over his shoulder, his brows going up for a moment in surprise as I carefully changed places with Mr. Bailey. The boat was much more stable with the weight of three men in it. I took hold of the oar handles, adjusting my hands until my grip felt sure, then tried to imitate what I had seen.

Theo's head remained turned as his arms rotated rhythmically. "The trick is to ensure the oar goes in like this." He slowed his movements so I could see the way the thinnest part of the oar entered the water first.

I twisted my own oars and followed his instructions, feeling the way the water dragged against them, forcing me to use my strength to counter its pull. Theo nodded approvingly as the oars emerged. My movements became more sure with each attempt until I matched the speed of Theo and the admiral in front of him.

Theo smiled at me, and I couldn't help but return it, thrilling in the way the wind blew against my face and the water rushed past us, drawing us ever nearer the ship.

When we arrived at the *Kestrel*, I was breathless but feeling strangely alive. We boarded the ship, which seemed much grander than it had from so far away. And to think, Theo would be captain of it all.

Admiral Bailey took Theo's attention, explaining the peculiarities he could expect to find upon the *Kestrel*, while Mr. Bailey and I trailed behind. I watched as the sailors moved deferentially to the other side of the ship to make way for the admiral and Theo, reminding me of when Theo had said being captain could be a lonely position.

Well, it was a position he was *choosing* to be alone in, so I did not have much sympathy for him at the moment. I had no intention of following him and the admiral around, listening to them as they spoke of Theo's future—the one I would play no part in—so I asked Mr. Bailey if we could stay on the upper deck.

He gladly assented, looking somewhat green. "The less I move about, the better."

We moved to the side of the deck, and I set my arms on the edge, looking out over the waves. I had no idea what ship Arthur and I would be taking tomorrow, but I doubted it would be as large or fine as this one. Theo would make a good captain of it. I had no doubt of that. I might be hurting inside at his rejection, but I hoped he would be happy on the *Kestrel*.

"What do you think now, Miss MacKinnon?" Mr. Bailey asked beside me. "Have I cured you of your desire to sail?"

I smiled and shook my head. "I'm afraid not." I wanted it more than ever. But the journey home to Scotland would have to be enough for me. And perhaps it would be. I would see my brothers and my childhood home, and perhaps I would be satisfied then.

But before I could go home, I had to discuss things with Mr. Bailey. And this was as good a time as ever. I took in a deep breath of the fresh, salty air, and turned toward him.

Chapter Eighteen

"Mr. Bailey?" My heart thrummed nervously inside me as he turned to look at me.

"Yes?"

"I . . . I need to speak with ye." Looking into his kind but pale face, my guilt surged again.

"Of course," he said, looking at me intently to show I had all my attention. "What is it?"

I rested my elbow on the edge of the ship, clasping my hands tightly as I considered how to phrase what I needed to say. He had not offered for me yet, so it felt presumptuous of me to speak of things as though he meant to. But I needed to be clear with him.

I let out an uncomfortable laugh. "I dinna ken how to say this." I straightened my shoulders and looked him in the eye. "I'm leavin'."

His brow knit. "Leaving?"

I nodded, watching his reaction carefully. "Back to Scotland."

His eyes searched mine for a moment. "When?"

"Tomorrow."

"I see . . . ."

I bit my lip, waiting to see what he made of this information. Would he think I had toyed with his affections? Played fast and loose with him? I had never meant to hurt him. And, in truth, I couldn't tell if he *was* hurt. He looked . . . pensive, not pained. But I needed to give him some explanation.

"Ye're kind, attentive, and a good man," I said, "and I consider ye my friend."

"But nothing more," he supplied.

I swallowed, not answering.

He smiled wryly. "Your heart is already engaged."

I did not answer immediately—didn't answer because I wished it wasn't true. Would my heart ever *not* be engaged?

"To Captain Donovan," he said softly.

I glanced down. How had he known? Was my lovesickness written on my face so plainly?

"I began wondering when the two of you were missing the other day," he explained, answering my unasked question. "Both of your shoes were covered in sand."

I tucked my lips in. Who else had noticed? And had they guessed at the nature of the meeting? "'Tis true that I regard Theo with great affection," I said. "But 'tis not that alone which takes me back home." I lifted my shoulders. "I havna been home in many a year. And I have some things to . . . resolve, I suppose."

He nodded. "I understand, Miss MacKinnon."

I looked into his eyes, trying to gauge whether he truly *did* understand, whether I had hurt him.

"I have a great regard for you," he said. "And I wish you nothing but the best."

I tried to smile and was certain it was a pitiful attempt. I would almost rather he railed at me than to take things so calmly and respectfully.

Theo and Admiral Bailey came down the steps from the quarterdeck, and I saw Theo's gaze land upon me.

"Mr. Bailey," I asked. "Will yer father be angry?"

He set his hand on mine, which were still clasped before me, and looked into my eyes. "You need not worry yourself over that, Miss MacKinnon. I will handle things with my mother and father."

I gave a rueful smile. "I rather think yer mother will be relieved."

He laughed but said nothing to counter me, which only confirmed that I was correct. It assuaged my guilt a bit, knowing I would not be causing tension between mother and son. Mr. Bailey would find a woman more suited to him than I. I was sure of that.

"And yer father?" I glanced at Admiral Bailey in discussion with Theo as he pointed up at the mainmast. "Will he change his mind about the captaincy?"

Mr. Bailey shook his head. "I will ensure that does not happen. Be at ease, Miss MacKinnon."

I took in a breath and nodded as the admiral and Theo turned to us, informing us that it was time to make our way back to the docks. I asked Mr. Bailey if I might row again—I needed an outlet for the strange mixture of emotion I was feeling now that I had accomplished the task that I had most dreaded.

Had I made a mistake? Once the strength of my feelings for Theo dulled, would I regret not marrying a man as good as Mr. Bailey?

No. It would not be fair to him for me to marry him when my heart was in the state it was now. He deserved better than that, and so did I. Who was to say, after all, whether we might come to resent one another for marrying under such circumstances—particularly when Lady Bailey had no fondness for me?

I rowed harder than ever, focusing again on the way the water rushed past, and we reached the docks much more quickly this time with the current in our favor. Diana, my brother, and

Admiral Donovan were waiting for us when we arrived. Arthur offered Admiral Bailey his hand to help him up to the dock.

When it was my turn to exit the boat, Theo was waiting for me, his hand extended just at it had been before. Mr. Bailey was hanging back in the boat—perhaps he had done so to ensure that Theo would be the one to assist me again. I could appreciate his good intentions even if they would only serve to make things more difficult for me in the end. Every touch with Theo sent a jolt to my heart that put its recovery farther and farther off.

It was decided upon that we would all take an hour to walk about the town before leaving back to Blackwick, and I sought Diana immediately, looping my arm into hers. We hadn't finished our conversation, and she already felt as though I had kept information from her.

Diana was accustomed to keeping a brisk pace even on a leisurely walk, and I was obliged to pull back on her so that I could tell her of my looming departure in private.

"Why?" she asked, looking slightly hurt. "Why now?"

"'Tis time for me to go home." I grimaced. "Years past time, I reckon."

"Do not be ridiculous, Elena." She glanced ahead of us and lowered her voice. "It is because of my idiot brother, isn't it?"

I shook my head, laughing wryly. "It feels like the right thing to do." I sent her an apologetic smile. "Perhaps you can come visit me in Scotland."

She tried to return the smile, but I could see how my news had dampened her spirits, and it brought tears to my eyes. Diana had been the only constant in my life since my arrival at Blackwick Hall.

"This is far from how I had hoped things would turn out," she said. "For the past two hours, I have been imagining having you as my sister." She perked up slightly. "You could marry Phineas. Or Valentine."

I gave a watery chuckle as her nose scrunched. "Perhaps not," she conceded. "The only romance in Phineas's life is with his books. And as for Valentine . . ." She raised her brows significantly. "He has far too *much* romance in *his* life."

I rested my head against hers as we walked. "We *are* sisters, Di. I'll always consider ye as one."

Diana was less gregarious on the journey back to Blackwick, but as Lady Bailey had much to say about our time in the port—complaints about the smells and people, among other things—we managed to arrive home without being obliged to enter the conversation too much.

"Well," Arthur said as he dismounted and I stepped down from the chaise. "I, for one, havna had my fill of this bonnie day. I intend to go for a wee stroll if anyone cares to join me."

After a bit of discussion about how much time remained until it would be necessary to dress for dinner, everyone agreed to join Arthur, and we took the path that led on the outer edge of the lawn. Everyone was eager to be in the outdoors after the rain we'd had.

Somberness overcame me as we promenaded and I thought on all the years I had spent here at Blackwick. I would miss much about it, but it was time to leave such dreams behind.

Theo, too, seemed more reserved than usual. He and Mr. Bailey walked together, and while he responded civilly to the man, there was a little *v* between his brows that told me his thoughts were elsewhere. How would he feel when he discovered I was leaving? Or that I was not to marry Mr. Bailey?

I shook myself. It did not matter what he thought or felt. It did not matter what *I* thought or felt. We had both made our decisions, and that was that.

"Does this go down to the water?" Arthur asked as we came upon the path that led to the cove.

"Yes," Diana said. "To the beach, rather."

"Ye have me convinced," he said, diverging from the one that led around the grounds of Blackwick to the path down to the cove.

Everyone followed, and I hung back for a moment, not certain whether I wanted to return to the cove or if I never wanted to see it again. Theo glanced at me, hesitating as though he might come ask me why I was not following. Was he remembering our moments here too?

For so long, I had thought of the cove as *my* place. How was it possible, then, that after just a few afternoons spent with Theo there, I had come to think of it as *our* place?

I took a decisive step forward. It would be wise to have a different memory than my kiss with Theo as the last one I had of the cove. Theo remained where he was, and I excused myself as I brushed past him, following behind the others.

I didn't have to look behind me to know he was there. His footsteps alerted me to the fact, but I imagine I should have known even without them. I seemed to always be aware of where he was in relation to me. Should I tell him that I would be leaving? What did it matter, really? Whether I left or not, he would be leaving soon as well.

By the time I reached the sand at the bottom of the path, the others had already begun walking the length of the shore. My eyes shot immediately to the cave at the other end of the beach. Were my creations still there, or had the tide finally come up with the storm and washed them away? Arthur seemed to be heading straight for the cave.

Picking up my skirts, I hurried along, trying to catch up with him in the front of the group. "Where are ye goin'?"

He pointed to the cave. "There."

"I dinna think we should go there, Arthur. It could be dangerous."

He chuckled. "This comin' from my wee sister who always insisted on swimmin' to the other end of the loch, rain or shine?"

I glanced behind us at Lady Bailey, whose brows were furrowed and her lips pinched together as she picked her way over the debris strewn across the beach. Well, she needn't worry about my shameless behavior anymore. She would soon know that.

We reached the edge of the cave, and I went up on my toes to see over the rocks to the place where my creations hid. They were intact, but for a few pieces which had slipped to the sand.

"What are those?" Lady Bailey said as she came up alongside me.

Arthur let out an incredulous chuckle and stepped over the nearest rock toward the little houses and crouched down. "*These*, my lady, are wee fairy houses." He was grinning widely, forearms resting on his knees as he surveyed them, oblivious to the effect of his comment on Lady Bailey, as always.

Arthur looked up at me as the others all gathered around. "I didna ken ye still made these, Lena."

Lady Bailey's head whipped around to look at me. All eyes, in fact, were upon me, and I wavered over how to respond for a moment. But what did I care for the opinion of Lady Bailey or her husband anymore? I would be on my way to Scotland soon.

"Just somethin' to pass the time," I said.

"Building houses for heathen creatures?" Lady Bailey said in incredulous shock.

"Och, the brownies can be verra kind when they fancy it," Arthur said without a trace of defensiveness. "Better take care they dinna hear ye speakin' ill of them, though. They can be feisty if upset." The way his smiling eyes glittered told me he was not entirely oblivious to how he was affecting her.

Admiral Bailey was looking more severe than ever beside his wife.

"I am shocked, Miss MacKinnon," she said. "Shocked, I tell you, to find that you engage in this sort of behavior. I feel very much deceived in your character."

"Come, Lady Bailey," Theo said, emerging beside me. "They are harmless."

She turned toward him, eyes wide, then looked up to her husband beside her.

"Harmless is certainly not the word I would use to describe such superstition," Admiral Bailey said.

"Indeed," Admiral Donovan commented. "I have seen it cause problems aboard many times."

Theo opened his mouth to reply, but I put a hand on his arm and shot him a warning look. The last thing I wanted was for him to run afoul of Admiral Bailey in defense of me. I needed no defense. I was tired of pretending to be the sort of woman of whom Lady Bailey would approve. Besides, perhaps the more I shocked her, the more relieved she and her husband would be that their son and I would not be making a match.

"It was quite enough to know that you had a tolerance for these hedonistic beliefs, Miss MacKinnon," said Lady Bailey, motioning to the houses.

"Mother," Mr. Bailey said, but he was cut off from speaking any further by a peremptory hand from his father.

Lady Bailey continued. "To know that you actively *practice* such beliefs yourself . . ." She shuddered, unable to finish.

It did not matter that I did not construct the houses with the expectation that brownies would come dwell in them, that they were merely a connection to a home I felt was slipping from my memory more and more each day, or that they provided peace and calm for me—none of that would matter to Lady Bailey.

She lifted her chin determinedly. "I can no longer in good conscience associate with you." She turned to her son. "And neither should you."

"Mother, surely this is an overreaction," Mr. Bailey said, clearly embarrassed by her behavior.

"Hardly," she replied. "I sensed from the beginning the

unwisdom of a connection between our family and Miss MacKinnon, and that suspicion has been borne out more than once."

I was determined not to allow her to ruffle me, but my anger rose all the same. "Ye dinna have to fret over that, my lady. I'm leavin' back to Scotland tomorrow."

She blinked, turning to her son, who gave a small nod, then shot me a look full of apology. I returned it, for I was certain this was not the way he would have chosen to reveal our discussion to his mother.

I felt Theo's eyes upon me, intent, as though he wished me to meet his gaze. But I did not.

"I should be preparin' for the journey." I curtsied. "If ye dinna mind, I'll excuse meself now."

I threaded my way through Admiral Donovan, Arthur, and Diana, and adopted a quick pace to the path. When I heard footsteps behind me, I closed my eyes in consternation. I hadn't the heart to speak with anyone now.

But it was only Arthur, and he said nothing as we made our way toward Blackwick Hall. If Lady Bailey had no desire to associate with me, I would make it easy for her. I would keep to my room until it was time for Arthur and me to leave.

Chapter Nineteen

I did not go down for dinner. I was not even hungry, truthfully. I was still too put out by the encounter at the cove.

Instead, I pulled out all the pins in my hair, letting it flow freely as Hitchen brought over my shift and dressing gown. Together, we began the work of readying my belongings for departure. I had borrowed a number of things from Diana over the years, and I set them on the bed until a large pile had accumulated, full of gloves, stockings, ribbons, and dresses.

"That will do for tonight, I think, Hitchen," I said when I began to feel tired and to wish for solitude. She nodded and left the room.

I stared at the pile—evidence of Diana's generosity over the years. Just as she had readily lent her lady's maid to me when I wished to look my best the night of Theo's arrival, she had never hesitated to lend or give me whatever I stood in need of. I had gained access to my own inheritance when I turned twenty-one, but given that my family's man of business was in Scotland and my brothers had been at war, it had been a difficult and time-consuming affair for me to draw upon it at need.

A knock sounded upon my door, and I stilled. Was it Arthur? What if it was Theo?

I glanced at the state of myself, ready for bed far before my normal hour except for my hair, which needed to be plaited.

"It is Di."

I let out a breath of relief and slight disappointment. What I was hoping Theo would come to say, I didn't know, but I hurried to open the door and let Diana in. She carried a tray with two plates, one holding the savory bits of dinner, the other an assortment of sweetmeats.

"Going to sleep already?" she asked as I closed the door behind her.

"Apparently not," I teased.

She surveyed the open trunks and the wardrobe, which was nearly bare.

"You truly mean to go, then," she said, setting the tray on the bedside table.

I nodded. "But not before I return all of this." I indicated the pile on the bed.

"Do not be ridiculous," she said. "Those were all gifts."

"Di," I said, overwhelmed with her kindness.

She smiled. "What? It is not so unselfish as you think. Perhaps you will not be so quick to forget me if I force you to take all of this with you."

I shot her an unamused look.

Diana was not one to linger over heavy emotions, though, and she sat down on the bed, looking at me with a glint of mischief in her eyes. "You were missed at dinner."

I gave something between a snort and a laugh. "I doubt that."

"*I* missed you," she said. "You abandoned me to entertain the Baileys and to put up with Father's pouting. He was far from pleased at Theo's absence."

"Absence?" I repeated, sitting beside her and taking a small tart from the tray.

"Yes, the revelation of your departure made him look as grim as my father generally appears. He was upset enough that the prospect of dinner conversation was unsupportable, I gather—I cannot blame him for that—and he went on a ride rather than join us."

I didn't respond, for I didn't know what to say.

We sat together on the bed until late in the night, reflecting upon our time at Blackwick and Mrs. Westwood's, until finally, our eyes began to droop with the need for sleep.

And yet, when Diana finally left, I found it difficult to achieve slumber. It was my last night at Blackwick Hall, and my mind was full of the past, distracted by questions about Theo and what he was thinking and feeling. Was he angry at me for not marrying Mr. Bailey? Would I ever see him again? The thought of a life devoid of Theo made me feel strange and hopeless, despite the prospect of going home.

When I woke in the morning, I was not well-rested, but with the things that still required packing, there was no time to attempt any more sleep. Perhaps I would do so on the ship. Hitchen assisted me with the final preparations, and we said a tearful goodbye to one another. She would stay behind, for England, not Scotland, was *her* home.

When the time approached for departure, I went downstairs to find Admiral Donovan, little relishing this final encounter. But he was far less foreboding than I had anticipated when I explained to him that I was leaving.

"I rather anticipated you might wish to leave back to Scotland once Arthur arrived."

I looked at him, trying to gauge his mood. "Ye're no' angry, then? That I'll no' be marryin' Mr. Bailey?"

He shook his head. "Admiral Bailey has as much as promised

my son the captaincy. All that remains is the formality of speaking with the other members of the Admiralty."

I swallowed, simultaneously grateful to avoid Admiral Donovan's ire and somber at the news of Theo's future. Securing his son's position seemed to have put him in an unusually placable mood. "That is wonderful news, sir."

"It is indeed." He looked at me, and his gray, bushy brows furrowed slightly. "I am sorry that I have not been a more present godfather, Elena. I suspect your brother will do a much better job of caring for you than I have."

"Nay, sir," I said. "Ye've given me a home and a family when I didna have my own to turn to. I'll always be grateful for that." I could feel my throat thickening and cleared it. Admiral Donovan was not the sort of man to appreciate emotion-filled conversations.

He rose from his desk and walked over to me. "It was my pleasure to do so. You have kept Diana company, too, for which I am grateful. I did not wish her to be neglected, and you have the sort of sense and decorum she so desperately needs in a friend." He took up my hand, clasping it within his. For him, such a gesture was tantamount to an embrace. "I wish you and your brother a safe journey back to Scotland. You are welcome at Blackwick whenever you wish to join us here."

I smiled and nodded, wondering if I ever *would* return here.

The Donovan family and Mr. Bailey gathered to bid Arthur and me farewell, though Theo, Admiral Bailey, and Lady Bailey were conspicuously absent. I preferred that the admiral and his wife keep their distance, but Theo's absence cut me at the heart.

"He has not come out except to meet with Admiral Bailey early this morning," Diana explained in a low voice as we embraced. "You mustn't heed him, Elena. He is merely my *stupid* brother, and you are far better off without him."

I nodded, offering a weak smile as we pulled apart. Perhaps Theo was wise to stay away. What could possibly be said?

My trunks were loaded into the Donovan's chaise, and, with a final look at Blackwick Hall, I stepped up into the carriage, and we were soon on our way.

Arthur tried to raise my spirits on the journey to Dover, and I made my best attempt at letting him believe himself successful, while inside, my heart hurt more than ever. Even the prospect of sailing was not sufficient to soothe me. My pain was still fresh, and in some ways, the thought of breathing the same sea air as Theo was like literal salt in my wounds.

We reached the same inn we had stopped at yesterday. Two servant boys there moved our belongings to the docks while Arthur and I took some refreshment in the inn to prepare us for our journey. I took but three sips of my coffee and two bites of the toast offered me, for my stomach was unsettled.

Once Arthur had finished his robust meal—mutton, eggs, toast, and two cups of ale—we made our way to the docks. I surveyed the bustle of the late morning and the mists which still hung about the waters under today's gray sky. My gaze went immediately to the *Kestrel* in the distance. Soon Theo would take command of it, and it would be sailing at sea rather than continuing as part of the Dover horizon.

"Which ship is ours?" I asked.

"That one there." He pointed, and as I followed the direction of the gesture, my eyes widened. It was the ship I had mentioned to Mr. Bailey yesterday. A number of men were hard at work on the deck, preparing her for departure.

I looked to Arthur, wondering if he was teasing me. "Truly?"

He nodded. "I received a message this morning informing me of a change of ship. Apparently the one we were meant to take sprang a large leak. Come." He led us to the gangway, and I followed him up the board, still baffled that, of all the vessels we might have boarded, this was the one which would take us home. It was a bit of balm to my heart.

I reached the top of the gangway where Arthur took to

conversing with one of the sailors, and I looked around, feeling a sudden buzz of anticipation for the journey. This might be my only chance to sail, and I wanted to remember everything.

"Elena," Arthur said, turning to me. "I slipped the communication I received this morning into your trunk when we reached the inn. Would you mind retrieving it? It seems there is a small problem. It is just up those stairs on the upper deck."

My stomach dropped, and the anticipation I had been feeling evaporated. Would we be left to kick our heels here in Dover for a few days while things were arranged? Now that we had left Blackwick and the Donovans behind, I was anxious to be home.

I nodded and made my way up the stairs, glancing between the slats at the small space beneath. Theo had said that Phineas often hid to read in just such a space.

Would every corner of the ship remind me of Theo somehow?

Our trunks and portmanteaux were stacked against the side of the deck, and I moved mine to gain access to my trunk. I took my reticule and uncinched it, but the key was not there.

My stomach dropped. How had I lost it? It had been here when we left Blackwick. I pressed my eyes closed and, in a fruitless gesture born of frustration, put my hands to the lid. Could nothing go right? I rattled it, blinking as the lid gave way to the force. It wasn't locked. Had Hitchen forgotten to lock it?

Grateful for her carelessness, I opened the lid and picked up the folded paper that sat atop my belongings.

I put a hand to the lid to close it, then stilled, frowning.

The letter said my name on the front. I stared at it for a moment in confusion, then turned it over and pulled it open.

It was short.

My dear Elena,
Welcome aboard the Alba.
Your servant,
Captain Donovan

I blinked, reading it again.

"I wanted to write you a full letter."

I whipped around and stood, finding myself facing Theo. He wore a well-fitted navy coat and a fresh, white cravat, his cocked hat tucked between his arm and his body, every bit of his clothing and his bearing asserting that he had command here. But his expression held a degree of caution and uncertainty.

"It was a bit of a scramble to purchase this ship and ready it for sailing in such a short amount of time, so I hope you can forgive the brevity of my letter."

"I dinna understand," I said.

He smiled slightly. "This is my ship now, Elena. The *Alba*. I bought it."

"Bought it?"

He smiled. "I have a fair bit of prize money to my name, you know."

I was struggling to keep pace with what he was saying. "But . . . what of the Navy? And the *Kestrel*?"

"I informed Mr. Bailey of my resignation this morning—and sent off formal notice of it too."

I stared. "Theo . . ."

"I am my own man now, Elena. With my own ship to captain as I will." His gaze became more intent. "I can choose who comes aboard." He took a step toward me. "I read my mother's journal when I returned home late last night—didn't sleep at all. You were right. She was most content on a ship, despite being ill. She didn't want to return to Blackwick. She wanted to be with her family." His expression became stricken. "If I had known, I would have taken her aboard with me. I swear it."

I nodded, for I believed him.

"If it weren't for you and Diana, she might have been truly miserable." He swallowed. "I don't wish to make the same mistakes my father made. Nor do I wish to live my life to please him anymore. I have tried that and found it does not suit me."

He took another step toward me. "I will take you to Scotland if that is what you wish. You deserve to see your home after all these years. In truth, I would like to see it too. And then, if you wish to stay, I will leave you there."

"But"—he swallowed, and his eyes grew almost pleading as he took my hands—"I hope more than anything I have ever hoped in my life, Elena, that after you have been home, you will come with me." He squeezed my hands. "And *stay* with me. I want you to sail with me on the *Alba*, and I want you to marry me."

I took in a shuddering breath, wondering if perhaps my lack of sleep was leading me to vain imaginations, things I had wished for but could never have. If this *was* a dream, it was a cruel one. This was too much like what I had imagined it would be when Theo returned from war. Better, in fact.

I looked down at his hands, holding mine. I could feel their warmth, their pressure. I could see every scrape and scar there. It couldn't be a dream.

The space between us grew smaller, and Theo's voice grew soft as his thumb ran along the back of my gloved hand. "Will you come? See the world with me? I cannot promise it will be glamorous or that there will be no discomfort. There shall be danger, even. But I *can* promise to stay by your side through it all—the good and the bad."

My heart pulsed with longing at his words, and I pulled one of his hands to my mouth, pressing a kiss upon it. "It is everything I have ever wanted."

Smiling with disbelief, he took my face in his hands and looked me in the eyes. "I think I have always loved you, Elena. I was so intent on pleasing my father, though, that I didn't recognize it for what it was." His gaze grew warmer. "But I know now."

"When did ye realize it?" For some reason, the thought that

it had only been my transformation into an English lady that was responsible was a lowering one.

"Slowly," he said ruefully. "I thought of you often at sea, wondered about you, missed you. I thought it was part of my homesickness, but it never went away. Ironically, I even considered writing to you—and now I dearly wish I had. Little did I know, it was *you* behind my mother's letters. You were there the whole time." His thumb rubbed my cheek softly. "I left you behind once, Elena, and I never wish to do so again."

"If you do, I shall call upon the brownies to haunt your every step."

His mouth drew up into a smile, and he pulled my face toward his, bringing our lips together. I wrapped my arms around him, crushing the letter in my hand against his back in an effort to draw him nearer, though he could never be near enough for my liking.

Cheering sounded around us, and we broke apart, my cheeks warming immediately at the sight of our audience. Amongst them, I recognized the man Theo had embraced yesterday, smiling brightly at us.

"Povey was instrumental in making all of this possible," Theo said. "He knows this ship in and out."

Arthur was clapping and walking toward us, a wide grin on his face. He came right up to us, then bent and picked up Theo's hat, brushing it off with a hand. It must have dropped during our embrace.

"If this carelessness is a reflection of how ye command a ship, Captain, I dinna ken if I care to go with ye." He handed the hat to Theo, who took it with a laugh.

"Ye kend?" I said to Arthur. Little wonder he had been so enthusiastic on the journey here despite my lackluster mood.

His smile was answer enough. He reached into his pocket and pulled out a key, answering the question I had had but entirely forgotten about in the past few minutes. He must have taken it while we were at the inn. "I *did* receive a letter this mornin' changin' our plans. I merely failed to tell ye who it came from."

I shot him a look. "I suppose I can forgive ye." I looked up at Theo beside me. His arm was about my waist, and he leaned over, kissing me on the forehead in a way that sent my heart into a mad flutter. It was so full of tender affection.

"Well?" Theo shouted at the sailors watching us, though his mouth was still drawn up in a smile. "What are you waiting for? We have some sailing to do. Back to work, boys!"

He held my hand, taking me with him as he gave orders. Meanwhile, I observed with fascination the sort of work that was required to ready a vessel for a journey.

Soon enough, the ship began to draw away from the docks, taking us farther from the coast, where white cliffs towered over the dark water.

Once everything was well in order, Theo led me by the hand to the side of the deck, standing behind me and wrapping his arms around me. "This is one of my favorite parts of sailing—watching the coast until it fades and disappears into the horizon."

I closed my eyes, reveling in the feeling of the wind on my face and Theo's arms around me, finally experiencing together what he loved and what I had long wished for.

"Oh," he said, pulling away from me. "One more thing."

I turned toward him, resting my back against the wood railing.

He pulled a paper from his coat, his smile growing teasing. "I thought we might read this together to pass some of the time on the journey."

My brows drew together, and I took the paper from his hand. It was old and worn, and I flipped it over. My eyes widened at the sight of Theo's name written in my own handwriting.

"I thought surely my father had got rid of it," he said. "He must have known somewhere inside that we were meant for each other, though."

"Ye havna read it yet, then?"

He shook his head.

I made to throw the letter out into the sea, but Theo caught my hand and secured my arm behind me, a playful smile in his eyes as he pressed up against me and looked down into my eyes.

"You do not wish for me to read it?" he asked.

"I dinna wish to humiliate meself," I replied.

"You mean to say that what you have written there does not accurately reflect what you feel now?"

I frowned at him. "Let me see." I turned away as I opened the letter and read the first lines. Some of it was still familiar, for certain phrases had haunted me for years. But now I had to bite my lip to keep from laughing—not at the sentiment behind the words but at how I had chosen to express them. It was funny how the past could change shape depending upon the present, how past joy could turn into pain or past pain into joy. This letter had held such power over me for so long. Now, I found that I *wanted* to share it with Theo. I wanted to share everything with him.

"Verra well." I turned back to him, only to find he had been right behind me, peering over my shoulder. I hit him with the letter, and he laughed, backing away from my reach.

"I hardly saw a thing," he said, holding up his hands in surrender. His smile grew teasing. "But, *are* you *languishing in misery, tormented by the bittersweet memory of my face?*"

I pulled my lips between my teeth to stifle my laughter. "That's hardly the most embarrassin' thing I said." I opened the letter again.

"Embarrassing?" He came up beside me and wrapped an arm about my waist again. "Your sentiments do you great honor, in my opinion."

"If that's what ye think, by the time ye finish readin' it, I'll be so full of honor, I'll burst."

He pulled me closer to him. "Then I shall hold you together."

I raised up on my toes to kiss him. I had a feeling that Theo and I would be holding each other together. And I wouldn't have it any other way.

Epilogue

"Elena."

I looked up from where I was helping one of the sailors with the rigging.

Theo stood a few feet away, attired in the fine apparel he wore only when going ashore—his dark blue coat, gray waistcoat, and white cravat. It was a sight that never ceased to steal my breath. If I had seen Theo thus when I had been fourteen, my foolish letter would have been the least of my worries—I might have followed him aboard his ship.

Smiling softly at me, he jerked his head toward the side of the deck. I finished with the rope and set it down, following him to the front of the main deck, just shy of the stairs, which afforded a view of what lay before the *Alba*. I squinted, looking toward the horizon where a mass of land was beginning to become more clear.

"India," he said. "Finally."

We had set out on our journey months ago, just after our wedding in Scotland, and we had known our fair share of difficulties en route, from storms to doldrums to a few days in the wrong direction. But we were finally here, and I looked with anticipation at the view. I was anxious for India—the smells, the sights, the people. And to experience it all with Theo.

"What do you most anticipate?" he asked.

I thought for a moment and smiled. "Algernon the Elephant," I said, referencing the one in his father's study I had nearly broken.

He chuckled and wrapped his arm about my shoulders, pulling me closer. "I should have known."

"*Will* we see an elephant?" I had heard tales of them in India, but one never knew what to believe of the tales told by sailors.

"I promise you shall have your elephant, my love." He kissed my hair. "India will be a bit different from Scotland, I think."

I turned toward him, taking him by the lapels and pulling him toward me. "'Tis a shame, for I *did* fancy Captain Donovan in Scotland."

"Not as much as I fancied *you* there." He ran his hand through my uncoiffed hair, then kissed me upon the lips.

Our time in Scotland had been some of the happiest days of my life, becoming reacquainted with my home while I showed it to the man I was to marry. Theo had been eager to see and do it all, from swimming across the loch nearest Benleith and eating bannocks to talking with the tenant farmers and milking the coos.

He had done it all with gusto, and a part of me had healed with each moment we shared there, culminating in our wedding. I no longer felt the need to hide my accent or my hair or anything about myself. Theo loved all of it, and I had come to love it too.

"Do ye miss the Navy?" I asked as the distant forms began to take shape where we would soon dock, including plenty of tall masts.

Theo shook his head. "I have no regrets. Perhaps I should not admit it, but I enjoy answering to myself—and you."

I had surmised as much. Theo was in his element on the

Alba. The crew worked hard for him, for they were treated *and* paid well by a man they loved and respected. Theo managed to walk the impossibly fine line between leader and friend, and I marveled at him every day. He took pains to teach me anything I wished to learn, and I wished to know it all. I wished to help on the *Alba*, to know its workings as well as the sailors.

Most of all, though, I marveled that Theo was mine and I was his and that this adventure, in all its difficulties and wonders, was our life.

"No regrets regardin' yer father, even?" I asked.

He shook his head again. "My father might be angry with me—in fact, I know he is, for Diana said as much in her last letter—but I know him, and deep inside, he cannot help but respect a man who knows his own mind. Besides, Diana has assured me she is working to slowly but surely soften him toward me."

I let out a little crow of laughter. "I should like to see that."

Theo wrinkled his nose. "Yes, I admit it was not terribly reassuring to read. *Soft* is not a word I would use to describe Diana's tactics. Perhaps I should write back and tell her not to make the attempt. But it is entirely possible she will forget all about it in her own frustrations with Father."

"Are they at each other's throats?"

Theo nodded, wry amusement in his eyes. "Whenever my father is not occupied with Navy business, that is. If there is anything I regret about being away from home, it is being unable to witness the battle likely to ensue when Diana and my father are set against one another in something."

I gave a little shudder, and Theo laughed, pulling me into his arms. "We may feel the repercussions all the way in India," I said.

He played with my hair—a habit he had developed whenever I wore it loose, which made me reluctant to ever wear it arranged in a way Mrs. Westwood would approve of. Perhaps there was more to her maxims about women's hair than I had given her credit for.

"Well, then," Theo said, "we shall have to hope she finds a man to take her away from Blackwick—one who inspires her to write four-page love letters, who sends her into the deepest melancholy whenever he leaves the room."

I smiled at his reference to my letter. We had come to quote it quite often to one another. Nothing was more effective at bringing both of us into a good humor.

But even with all those words I had written, dramatic and besotted as they were, they did not come close to conveying the way I felt about Theo now. "I canna imagine Diana fallin' into a melancholy over a man. And it seems a great deal to hope that *two* men worthy of a letter like mine could exist on this earth."

He gave a little chuckle, looking at me in the way that made my knees weak and my heart race. "I love you, Elena."

And he kissed me like he meant it.

THE END

Other Titles by Martha Keyes

The Donovans
Unrequited (Book .5)
The Art of Victory (Book 1)
A Confirmed Rake (Book 2)
Battling the Bluestocking (Book 3)

Sheppards in Love
Kissing for Keeps (Book 1)

Tales from the Highlands Series
The Widow and the Highlander (Book 1)
The Enemy and Miss Innes (Book 2)
The Innkeeper and the Fugitive (Book 3)
The Gentleman and the Maid (Book 4)

Families of Dorset Series
Wyndcross: A Regency Romance (Book 1)
Isabel: A Regency Romance (Book 2)
Cecilia: A Regency Romance (Book 3)
Hazelhurst: A Regency Romance (Book 4)

Romance Retold Series
Redeeming Miss Marcotte (Book 1)
A Conspiratorial Courting (Book 2)
A Matchmaking Mismatch (Book 3)

Standalone Titles
Host for the Holidays (Christmas Escape Series)
A Suitable Arrangement (Castles & Courtship Series)

Goodwill for the Gentleman (Belles of Christmas Book 2)

The Christmas Foundling (Belles of Christmas: Frost Fair Book 5)

The Highwayman's Letter (Sons of Somerset Book 5)

Of Lands High and Low

A Seaside Summer (Timeless Regency Collection)

The Road through Rushbury (Seasons of Change Book 1)

Eleanor: A Regency Romance

About the Author

Whitney Award-winning Martha Keyes was born, raised, and educated in Utah—a home she loves dearly but also dearly loves to escape to travel the world. She received a BA in French Studies and a Master of Public Health, both from Brigham Young University.

Her route to becoming an author was full of twists and turns, but she's finally settled into something she loves. Research, daydreaming, and snacking have become full-time jobs, and she couldn't be happier about it. When she isn't writing, she is honing her photography skills, looking for travel deals, and spending time with her family. She lives with her husband and twin boys in Vineyard, Utah.

Made in United States
North Haven, CT
11 February 2024